Echoes

of

His Mercies

By

Ronna M. Bacon

ISBN 978-1-989699-36-2

Lamentations 3

22 Through the Lord's mercies, we are not consumed, because His compassions fail not.

23 They are new every morning; great is Your faithfulness.

NKJV

Table of Contents

Chapter 1

Brushing off the fallen tree trunk, Grady Andrew Michaels dropped to a sitting position, his long legs stretched out in front of him as he drew off his cap and wiped his brow with the sleeve of the blue, white, and black plaid cotton shirt he wore. It was hotter than he had expected it to be in the forest, more humid as well.

His deep gray eyes searched the clearing, a favourite one of his, for something off. He could feel it, he thought, before he shrugged out of his backpack and reached inside for the bottle of water, uncapping it and drinking deeply. He brushed at the dark brown curls that always insisted on drooping over his forehead, even though he kept them cut short. Yes, he decided, something is definitely wrong here, and I don't know what.

He finally capped his water bottle and stuck it away, his eyes closing for a moment as he listened to the sounds of nature ringing and singing in his ears. Grady thought that he was most content when he was out in the forest, which is why he had chosen the occupation he had in forestry. He loved being able to walk the forest trails, assessing the trees around him, watching for the wildlife and their habitats, and just communing with God. That is where he felt closest to Him.

Shrugging into his backpack once more, Grady rose, intent on finding the trail of the deer that had been wounded by a hunter in the last few days. Illegal hunting at that, Grady thought. He inwardly fumed for a moment before he shook his head. It didn't matter that this was private land and signed as such. People still hunted, taking the chance of not being caught.

He paused, his head tilting for a moment. No, that was definitely a human voice he could hear, humming or singing low. A feminine voice. Now, who would that be out here? He walked cautiously forward, his eyes searching before he saw her. He stopped, not quite sure what she was doing.

Grady finally approached her, standing a few feet away from her, waiting for her to turn and acknowledge him. When she didn't, he cleared his throat and then opened his mouth to speak.

"Ssh! I know you're there. You sounded like a herd of elephants tromping this way! Now, be quiet!" Her voice was low and melodious, fascinating him.

Finally rising to her feet, her hands cupped together, she glared up at him, not seeming to mind that he towered over her, being six foot three. He watched, amusement dancing in his eyes, as she stomped towards him.

"Do you mind? I was trying to rescue this little one and you almost made it run." She opened her hands enough to show him a small rabbit. "It has a broken leg. I was out here, trying to research the plants, when I found it."

"This is private land, you know." Grady was at a loss for words, totally unusual for him. He studied her deep auburn hair she had drawn back into a ponytail.

Her curiously coloured green eyes reminded him of the depths of a lake he favoured for fishing.

"I know it is. I have permission to be here." She continued to glare at him. "But that still doesn't explain why you are here." She continued to cradle the small animal, a finger stroking along its back.

A sudden move on the rabbit's part had it flying from her hands and disappearing into the tall grass and weeds. A dismayed cry broke from her as she spun, searching for it, parting the grasses. Grady watched for a moment before he too began to search.

"I don't think we'll find it." He finally stood back to his full height, pulling his cap down further over his face to block the sun.

"I know. He'll become fodder for some other critter." Her hand raised as if she expected him to comment. "I know. I know. It's the chain of life."

"That it is. It doesn't make it easier when you are trying to help out a critter." Grady looked around, suddenly uncomfortable. "Listen? Are you okay here? I can stay."

She looked up at him once more, a frown appearing between her eyes before she shrugged. "I have no idea. So far, I have been." Her gaze drifted past him and a scream broke from her.

Grady stared at her for a moment, before he started to turn. A sudden tackle by a heavy body took him down, the breath leaving his body as he lay stunned. He was vaguely aware of another scream from the lady before he was hauled to his feet and then shoved forward. He felt her arm come around him to help steady him before they were forced to walk forward. Grady gradually steadied on his feet, his eyes straight ahead, his mind racing as to what had just happened.

They were eventually shoved into a cave, with one of their captors standing in the entrance, his back to them, as he watched the three other men who were with him gather brush and sticks, preparatory to starting a fire.

Grady dragged his companion to the back of the cave, sinking to a sitting position and pulling her down with him. A hand rested on her arm, keeping her still.

"Do you know these men?" His voice was low.

She nodded. "Unfortunately, I know one of them. Dad had to fire him a couple of months ago for stealing from him and for illegal hunting." She stared at the man in the doorway. "I think that one there is related to him."

Grady shifted so he could watch her face before shooting a glance at the man in the doorway.

"Illegal hunting? That's why I was out here today. We had reports of that and that there was a deer injured I needed to find."

She stared at him before a hand came up to cover her mouth.

"You're him."

"I'm who? What do you mean?" His voice was still low, barely audible, but definitely holding a puzzled tone in it.

"You're Grady Michaels, from that private forestry company. Dad said you would be around."

His gaze had shifted to watch the entrance, but at her words, he spun back to face her.

"Your dad? Just who is your Dad?"

"Garett MacDermott. Did you not know that? You're on his land."

Grady sat back, his gaze still fastened on her. "You're Eineen. His daughter."

"I am, and it's pronounced A-neen." She stared at the man, watching as he had shifted to look back at them. "I know this cave. There's another entrance we can take to get out of here. I grew up playing around here, with my brother."

"Now, your brother I know. We were in school together." Grady sank back. "How far along the cave is the entrance?"

"About fifty feet. We have to wait until it's darker in here. I can find it, I know. I've done it before in the dark."

Time passed, the dusk closing down on them. Eineen shivered slightly from the dampness in the cave. Grady hesitated and then wrapped an arm around her, drawing her closer to him and the warmth of his body. Eineen stiffened for a moment and then gratefully leaned against him, her eyes not moving from the light outside.

Finally, she stood cautiously, her hand reaching for Grady's as he too rose, taking one last look at the entrance and then leading him away, down a tunnel and then another tunnel until she reached the room she wanted. He looked around as best he could in the dark, not willing to let go of her hand.

"You need to let me go, Grady. Grab the back of my shirt. I just need to orient myself, and I have." A low gleeful cry broke from her as she found the crack she wanted and pulled at it.

To his surprise, the wall moved forward just enough so that they could enter. She reached behind him and pulled the wall back.

"Did that really happen?" He was dumbfounded for a moment.

"It did. Dad used to play here when he was young. My grandfather thinks it was part of a smuggling route." She headed away from him, feeling his grasp at her shirt as she did so.

They finally emerged into the late dusk of the falling night. She paused once more, listening before pointing to a trail.

"If we follow that trail, it will bring us out near my home. I have a cabin out here."

Grady's hand stopped her. "Before we go any further, I want to pray. I don't think we're done with them yet."

"Oh, I know for a fact we aren't. But please, go ahead. I sense that we are still in danger and I don't like it one bit."

Grady suddenly grinned, amused at the grumpiness of her tone. "You don't, eh? Okay. Let's pray and then move on out."

Grady's prayer helped to calm Eineen's rapidly beating heart. She had never felt fear like this before. She knew the men were stalking her, for what reason, she didn't know. Her father had warned her just that very morning to be on the alert, that he was trying to arrange security for her, and would she just please move home for now? He didn't think she was safe where she was living.

She had shrugged at his words and told him he was a worrywart and that she would be just fine. Now, she thought, those very words are coming back to haunt me. Dad was right. Something is going on out here.

Eineen stepped forward, trusting her memory of a trail she had not walked in over a year, finding the ground suddenly not there. A small scream broke from her as she lost her balance, Grady's mad grab for her catching her arm, but taking him forward at the same time. The couple plunged over the edge of the trail, tumbling down the slope, their bodies not missing the rocks, branches, and bushes as they did so, before rolling over and over to land near a small stream, to lie motionless. Grady sprawled facedown, one arm tucked under him, the other hand reaching for Eineen. Eineen lay a few feet away, on her side, dirt and blood covering her face, her hair a tangled mess around her face.

Silence reigned for a while before the night critters, insects and birds crept out, to study the two strange beings that had invaded their world and disturbed him. They decided they were no harm to them and the night became alive again as only nature can make it so.

Chapter 2

Pacing the clearing in front of his daughter's cozy log cabin, Garrett MacDermott studied the sky and then twisted his wrist to study his watch. Eineen should have been home by now, he thought. No, long before this. She was usually very careful about roaming around in the woods at night.

He sighed, his phone out to study his text messages. No, he hadn't had one from her but there was a number from his son, Eames. Garrett shook his head. He would have to call Eames, and if Eineen showed up at the same time as Eames, she would not be happy. And when Eineen was unhappy, she made sure everyone knew. Her parents had worked with her over the years, and she had gotten better, but lately, Garrett thought, something has triggered this attitude again. He would likely be needing to speak with her.

"Dad?" Eames' voice was rushed.

"Eames? Where are you?"

"Just about at Eineen's. Why?"

Garrett circled the cabin, his eyes straining through the dark, hopeful to see his daughter walking towards him. Lord, please? She's my only daughter, my little girl. Please, dear Lord, keep her safe. Bring her home tonight and now. And then, he prayed once more. Forgive me, Lord, for telling just what You should be doing. You are in control. Wherever Eineen is, please keep her safe.

———

"Dad? Are you there?" Eames' voice sounded worried, breaking up slightly with his travels through the trees. "I am. Just praying. I have a bad feeling, Eames. Eineen is not home, and she had planned to be. She had an article she was working on, she said, that needed to go to the editor tomorrow. Unless she finished it already. I can't tell from the papers scattered over her desk."

"Wait! Dad, did you say scattered over her desk?" Eames parked his truck, keyed it off, and pulling the key, pushed open his door to spring from the seat and run towards his father, his phone going into his pocket on the way. "Dad? That's not Eineen. She's too tidy."

Garrett stared at his son. "You're right. It's not her." He spun, running towards the cabin, his feet crunching on the fallen leaves and small sticks under them. The door hit the wall from the force of its opening as Garrett and Eames entered on a run, sliding to a stop near Eineen's desk.

"Dad? This mess? That's not Eineen. Someone has been searching through her papers, but why?"

"I have no idea." Garrett reached to straighten them, pulling back his hands before he touched them. "She won't like it but I need to call this in. Someone has been in here."

"They have, Dad." Eames stepped back to the door, bending so he could study the lock. "It's been jimmied. And it's a good lock."

Two hours later, Garrett looked up from where he had perched himself on a rocker, his eyes on the officer approaching him.

"Sam?"

Samuel Douglas shook his head. "They wore gloves, Garrett. We could find no prints other than likely Eineen's and your family's. Has she had any friends up here recently that we need to contact?"

Eames shook his head. "No, she hasn't. She told me that she needed some space and some quiet. Just why she phrased it that way, she refused to say. I know she has been looking over her shoulder lately, almost as if she was being watched or followed. When I asked her, she just shrugged, told me to never mind, and walked away."

"Eames? You never said anything." Garrett rose, his hand going to his son's shoulder.

"There wasn't much to say, Dad. She wouldn't say anything, but I know Eineen. Something has been bugging her." Eames rubbed at his cheek, his hand rough against the end-of-day stubble. "I tried, Dad. I really did. She just wouldn't tell me."

Garrett shook his head. "She's always been independent, more so than you. We've struggled all her life with that, Eames." He turned to stare towards the forest. "I just wish I knew where she was right now."

"Did she say where she was heading? I can head out there as soon as it's light." Eames watched his father closely, seeing the stress and worry he was trying so hard to hide.

Dawn had just barely cracked through the remnants of the night sky, sending brilliant rosy beams to lighten the darkness when Eames was on his feet, shrugging into a sweatshirt and lifting his backpack. He turned briefly to study his father, who still slept, the worry and stress of the night still weighing him down in slumber.

Eames stood on the back porch for a moment, adjusting the straps of the backpack, letting his eyes adjust the lightening of the sky. He looked up with a frown, noting the dark clouds moving in. Please, Lord, no rain? Not until I have found Eineen and brought her home safely.

He moved away from the cabin, not quite sure which way to move, but trusting that his request to his Lord would lead him aright. Eames paused after he had walked for about an hour, a frown on his face, before he reached for a baseball cap, to stare at it as he held it in shaking hands. It was Eineen's favourite cap. It was here, but just where was she? He spun in a circle, his eyes probing the forest and trees and brush around him, not seeing her. He called her name, walking forward as he did so, before he once more stopped, a frown on his face.

Eames stooped to reach for the phone that lay in front of him. It wasn't his sister's, that he knew. Her case had pictures of her favourite flowers on it. The one he held was a soft brown leather case, a man's, he thought. Now, who would be out here? Eames' thoughts raced, in keeping with the rapid beating of his heart, wild speculation in place.

The soft chiming of his phone startled him, causing him to almost drop the phone he held.

"Eames? Whereabouts are you?" Garrett's voice echoed over the phone, concern, and fear for both his children contained in it.

"Near the caves, Dad. I found Eineen's cap."

"Her cap?" Garrett's raised before it lowered back to its normal even tenor. "No sign of her?"

"None, Dad. But a short way from it, I found a phone. It's not hers. It looks like a man's."

"A man's? Can you open it?"

Eames had tried, but the screen was locked. "I have a business card tucked inside. Why! It's Grady's card. This must be his phone. But where is he?" Eames spun in a circle, not seeing anything that would alert him.

"Grady? He was to be out there yesterday. I talked to his employer. He was coming out to search for that wounded deer. They must have met up. Where are they, though?"

"I am heading towards the caves, Dad. Can you drive around and meet me on the old logging trail?" Eames heard the sound of a door slamming and then a truck door opening and closing. "I'm on my way. Be careful, Eames. We have no idea what has happened."

"I know, Dad. I know." Eames pocketed his own phone, continuing to stare down at Grady's. A friend, he thought, I haven't seen much of in the last few

years, and I have been remiss in that. Lord, please?
Keep them safe.

Chapter 3

Ducking his head to study the ground outside of the caves, Eames drew in a deep breath. A fire had been here, he thought, and just within the last twenty-four hours. He peered into the cave, and then entered, walking carefully to the side, studying the cave floor. Eineen, you've been here. I recognize the tread on your boots. And is that Grady with you?

He followed her tracks, seeing where the pair had sat, and then walked along the tunnels, reaching the same wall that Eineen. He pried it open, stepped through, bringing the wall closed behind him. He traced their steps, just catching himself in time from going over the same edge over which Eineen and Grady had tumbled. His heart in his throat, he grabbed onto a nearby sapling and leaned over carefully, fear coursing through him as he saw the broken brushes and shrubs and the path that the couple's tumbling bodies had taken.

Eames ran for the path he knew was there, running down it as quickly as he could, sliding in a lot of spots, his hands reaching out for whatever handholds he could find. Glancing up, he oriented himself to the edge and then thrust his way through the dense underbrush, suddenly emerging to a small clearing on the edge of a stream. He stood, dumbfounded that he could not see them, and spun again in a circle. I'm doing that a lot today, aren't I, Lord?

He pulled out his phone, sighing with frustration. No service or at least not enough that he could call for help. Eames walked carefully around the area, seeing other footprints. More, he though? Please, Lord, let them be from someone who has come to help, not to harm.

He followed for a while before he had to give up, the footprints lost in the water of the stream. Even searching along both banks didn't lead him to where they had come out of the water. And the water was too shallow for even a canoe.

Eames turned and headed for the logging road, his thoughts tumbling over one another. How to tell his parents, he thought, how do I do that? He looked up to see Garret striding towards him, hope on his face.

"Eames? Did you find them?" Garrett stopped, reading aright on the look on his son's face. "You didn't find them?"

"I found where they went over the edge of the trail behind the caves. They weren't alone in the caves. There were, I would say, four men with them. I don't like that, Dad."

"Nor do I." Garrett paused, torn, wanting to go to where Eineen had last been, but knowing they needed to bring in the authorities. "Would you say they weren't with them of their free will?"

"I would say that, Dad. It looks as if Eineen, and if it was Grady, were shoved into the cave. Eineen led them out, but the trail seems to have crumbled under them. I could see the path they went down the slope."

"And no sign of them at the bottom?"

"Not really. I mean, the area is torn up a bit. The thing is, Dad, there were other footprints. I can't tell if they were the same as the men who took them or someone else. I lost the track in the stream."

Three hours later, Garrett and Eames watched as Sam walked towards them once more, a shuttered look on his face.

"Sam?" Garrett's quiet voice sounded loud in the silence of the forest.

"Garrett? What was she doing out here? And who is that who was with her?"

"She has been studying some plants over the summer, for a project, she said. And we think it was Grady Michaels with her. Eames found his phone near where he found Eineen's cap."

"Grady Michaels? Okay, so that rules out him as a suspect." Sam paused, not quite sure what to say next. "We're searching, Garrett. They're bringing in the K-9 units, but frankly? I'm not sure if they'll be able to pick up much. It's like Eames said. The tracks disappeared."

"But how?"

"That we can ask them when we find them. For now, I would suggest that you two head back to Eineen's cabin. We'll be here for quite a while." His hand went up as Garrett protested. "It's better. That way, if she shows up there, you'll be able to let us know."

Garrett stared down at his hand, watching as his fingers moved one against the other, a habit that he had when he was deeply disturbed.

He finally raised his eyes, a sigh heaved from him, it seemed almost from his toes, before he nodded. He turned, his movements slow and weighted, the burden of worry about his daughter heavy on him.

Eames watched as his father walked away before he spoke.

"What didn't you say, Sam?" Eames kept watching his father walk towards the truck.

Sam shrugged. "I've known you since you were small, Eames, both you and Eineen. I have been friends with your parents since we were small. I don't know what happened to them after they went over the edge and tumbled down the slope."

He paused, knowing that he would have to be honest with his young friend. "We have heard rumours of a gang in the area, but just what they are up to, we haven't been able to determine."

"And you think Eineen and Grady are in their hands? How bad?"

Sam shook his head this time. "That we don't know, Eames, and that is what is worrying me. If your sister and your friend are in their hands, we really don't know what will happen." He turned himself to watch Garrett standing by the truck, arms extending across the hood, watching the forest. "He's waiting for her to walk out on her own."

"He is. Listen, Sam, I'm staying at Eineen's for now. Just so someone is there. Dad?

He'll have to head back and find Mom and talk to her. I know they talked last night." Eames shook his head. "I'm sorry, Sam. I just wish this hadn't happened."

Sam's hand rested on Eames' shoulder. "It has. Just don't lose sight of the fact that God is in control. And that He is faithful to us in all things."

"And great is that, isn't it? Just like the Scriptures state. Did you know those verses are Eineen's favourites?"

"No, I didn't. Hang onto them, Eames." Sam turned as he heard his name called and with a final squeeze of his hand to Eames' shoulder, turned and headed back towards the stream.

Chapter 4

A week had passed since their tumble down the slope.

Grady had roused a few hours after it had happened, his eyes blinking open to darkness, the night sounds in his ears.

He shoved up with one hand, his arm straightening and then shaking as he braced himself with it, the other arm that had been under him tucked close to his body. He had taken deep breaths, trying to clear his lungs and his head, not quite accomplishing that feat with his head. Grady shifted enough so that he could sit, waiting for a moment to steady himself, assessing what all hurt, or rather, he thought, what didn't hurt.

He glared up the slope to the top, unable and unwilling to believe he had tumbled down it. There had been someone with him, hadn't there?

He spun where he sat, his eyes sliding closed as his head spun faster than his movement. He saw the dark form on the ground near him and then he scooted closer to it, his attempt to rise thwarted by his head. He reached out a hand, feeing the rising and falling of the back of the person.

Grady gently rolled the person to its back, his hand tangling in long hair. A lady, he thought? I don't remember meeting a lady out here. Then, his memory sharpened and he drew in his breath. Eineen! This was

Eames' sister, Eineen. He remembered then their conversation and the assault that had led to them being taken captive. But who and why?

His next thought was how to get her out of there.

His arm was not useful, he decided, but he would carry her somehow. His ears picked up soft movement that stilled the sounds around him.

Grady rose to his feet, a hand to the tree near him to balance himself, his eyes straining to look into the night. He jumped as a body appeared suddenly beside him and then two more did.

No words were exchanged. The three men, as it was men who had appeared so suddenly out of the dark, simply motioned for him to pick up Eineen. He hesitated, knowing it would be difficult before he bent and scooped her up, one of her arms around his shoulders, before he straightened once more, waiting for his head to clear before he followed the first man, knowing that the two others were behind him.

Three hours later, Grady stumbled to a halt, barely able to stay upright, his arms tightening around Eineen so he didn't drop her, his blurry eyes seeking shelter. He looked again, seeing the cabins backed into the trees, invisible from the air, and almost invisible from the ground unless you knew they were there.

A shove on his shoulder had him moving forward, directed to a small cabin in the middle of the group, and then a shove on the same shoulder sending him through the door, unable to keep to his feet. Grady twisted as he fell, protecting Eineen as much as he was able to, his body slamming heaving on the dirt floor, where he lay, the breath knocked from him, dark spots skittering in front of his eyes.

The door shut solidly and he heard the clasp of a lock being clicked shut. His eyes closed for a moment as he laid his head down, his arms still tight around Eineen, taking a moment to catch his breath and clear his head. He finally moved to lay her down on the ground, standing and then searching the cabin for any way to escape and finding none.

Grady turned back to the room, walking over to the only bunk, the only furniture in the tiny cabin, and felt it. It was dry, he thought, which is good. He turned, bending over Eineen and lifting her carefully, finding that she was starting to rouse.

Seating her on the side of the bed, he crouched in front of her, his hands holding hers, watching carefully as she roused more and more.

"Eineen? Can you talk to me?" He smothered a grin at the glare he was given.

"I would if I knew just exactly who you were." She sighed. "I'm sorry. That was not nice of me. Where am I?"

"I'm not too sure. They made us walk a good two to three hours, I think, from the cave."

"Cave? What cave?" Eineen stared at him, a frown on her face. "Just who are you?"

"I'm Grady Michaels. A friend of your brother's. Your Dad asked me to find a wounded deer yesterday. Don't you remember?" Grady was puzzled, a frown on his own face.

Eineen shook her head, her eyes sliding closed. "What did you make me do that for?" She opened one eye and squinted at him. "I don't know a Grady Michaels. And I don't have a brother. Not that I know of."

"What's your name?"

"What do you mean, what's my name?"

"Just that. What is your name?" Grady's heart sank as he realized that she was struggling with that very fact.

Lord, he prayed, help her to remember.

She's the only one between us who knows where we would be and how to get out of here.

"Of course I know my name." Her brow furrowed as she fought her memories, trying to make it through the block that was there. She finally looked back up at him, tears in her eyes. "I can't remember. Why can't I remember?"

"It's okay." Grady stood, his hand reaching for her. "Here, head into the little washroom. You should be able to clean up a bit. I'll be right over by the door." He turned, moving to stand beside the door, his back to her.

Eineen stared at him, her brow still furrowed, before she rose and scurried into the small bathroom, finding a rough towel handing on the back of the door. She doused her face in cold water, finally standing, staring at her image in the mirror, not recognizing herself.

—

29

God, I don't know if I believe in You, but something tells me I do. I need Your help right now. I don't remember who I am, but I am so scared. Please, Lord?

Feeling at her pockets, Eineen pulled a phone from one, staring down at it, before she glanced at the door. She burst through it, heading for Grady across the few feet that separated them. Grady spun, worried at her sudden emergence and simply held out his arms, Eineen springing into them, her free hand grasping at his shirt.

"Eineen? What happened?"

"I have this. I don't recognize it."

"A phone? Good. I lost mine somewhere." Grady walked her backward until her legs hit the edge of the bunk and she sank down, her eyes on him, her hand extending the phone.

"You want me to take it?" At her nod, he sank down beside her, reaching for her phone. "Do you have the password for it?" He had discovered it was password protected.

She sighed. "No, I don't remember. That doesn't help up."

Grady's heart broke for her. Here they were, stuck in the middle of nowhere, held hostage by who knew who, Eineen couldn't remember who she was, and he had a phone that he would like to use for help, only he couldn't, simply because Eineen could not remember the password.

Lord, this would be a good time to show Your compassion and faithfulness and help Eineen to remember. But then, again, You have a reason for this, only I wish You would let us in on that.

31

Chapter 5

It was almost dark that day when the lock clicked open and the door slammed back against the wall to allow a hulking shape of a man to enter, his hair and beard long and unkempt. He stared at both Eineen and Grady as Eineen shrank back against him, his arm tight around her, his eyes steady on the man in front of him, catching sight of the three men who had herded them to this very clearing standing grouped in a half-circle behind him.

"Out." When the young couple didn't move, his voice raised and he shouted at them. "Out! You move when I say move." The building seemed to shudder at the violence and force of the shouted words.

Grady's arm stayed around Eineen as he walked carefully forward, his eyes not leaving the man as he backed out of the door. This must be the leader, Grady thought. Well, Lord, now what? How do we get away?

They stood, her hand tight in his, watchful, seeing additional forms moving towards them, men and women, and a few small children, all ill-kempt in appearance. Eineen moved as close to Grady as she could, not liking the way she was being watched. Grady's hand tightened on hers, in an effort to reassure her, but he knew that it wouldn't take much for him to go down and leave Eineen at the mercy of the people her.

The leader stood in front of him. Grady drew in a deep breath. He recognized him. Mac Duffy. His employer had warned him about this man, had told him not to engage him, but to retreat and let the police deal with him. He watched carefully as Mac swayed in front of him, the effects of an all-day drinking binge obvious.

Suddenly, Grady felt hands on him, tearing him away from Eineen, hearing her cry of horror as she turned and tried to get to him, to be forced away from him. Grady's arms were held in iron grips as he struggled to free himself, to no avail.

Eineen whimpered in fear as the man approached her, even though she kept backing away, heading towards where she knew Grady was standing. She could hear his mutters to let him go. She finally backed right into him, feeling the solid strength of his body behind her.

The leader stopped short of her, a hand reaching out to touch her hair, causing her to turn her face away from him and burrow it as much as she could against Grady.

The leader gave a harsh laugh, causing the same kind of laughter to come from the men around him.

"It's not going to do you any good, little lady.

He can't help you." Mac turned and stomped away, only to stop and spin, returning to stand in front of her. "I have a bone to pick with your father. You're not leaving here. Not today. Not tomorrow. Not ever." He stomped away, leaving her tight to Grady, who had frozen at the man's words.

What does he mean, Grady wondered? I have to get her out of here. He means her no good. He felt the hands loosen somewhat on his arms before they were both shoved forward and back into the cabin.

The same situation went on half a dozen times in a day, every day. Grady could tell that it was wearing Eineen down. He watched as she slept, huddled into as small a ball as she could curl.

He slept, back to the door, not willing to let anyone in unless he was awake. He feared for her. He saw the looks and heard the whispered comments from the men. He had to get her out of there, only there didn't seem to be a way. He had searched the cabin thoroughly, finding nothing he could use as a weapon and no way that they could escape.

On the seventh day, things had come to a head. Eineen had not heard the comments directed towards her. Grady could see that she was retreating into herself, not rousing as readily when he shook her awake, sleeping more and more. He had to get her out that night. If he didn't, the leader planned to make her part of his group permanently. He just could not let them do that.

A quiet scrape and then tap at the window had him on his feet, cautiously approaching. He peered out into the gathering dusk, surprise on his face to see one of the women there, Mac's woman, if he recalled rightly. He doubted that she was his wife.

She beckoned him forward, showing him a key that she had secreted in her hand, before pointing to the door. Grady nodded, turning quickly to move to the bed, standing for a moment staring down at Eineen, before he gathered her into his arms and headed for the door, reaching for their packs with a couple of fingers.

He waited as the door swung open and then the woman appeared, beckoning him silently to follow her, the door closed and locked behind her. She pointed to the forest, miming that she would be with him in just a few moments before she ran for her cabin, returning the key to Mac's key chain, watching closely as he slumbered in his drunkenness.

She turned and ran for the woods, her eyes watching that she was not spotted. She touched Grady on the shoulder, causing him to jump and almost drop Eineen. She had the packs in her hands and was moving rapidly away from him before he could even gather his thoughts, his feet automatically following, his head turning every few minutes to listen for anyone following or tracking them.

The woman stopped at a deeper creek, her hand dropping the packs into a canoe.

"Can you do this?"

"What? Paddle a canoe?" At her nod, Grady shrugged. "It's been a while. Where does it lead?"

"It will lead you to safety. It's a full moon tonight and you'll have lots of light. Now, you need to move." She thrust a paper at him. "Here. Find this man. He's a minister I know. Make sure you marry this girl tonight or tomorrow at the latest. If you don't, it will go bad with her if Mac ever gets his hands on her again." She was gone before Grady could ask another question. His quiet thank you wafted through the air before he turned.

Grady carefully lowered his burden into the canoe, shifting the packs to let her lie as flat as she could. He stood for a moment, head turned, before he shrugged. He could hear no one. He felt for Eineen's phone. It was still in his pocket, but he didn't know how much of a charge could be left, even if he knew the password to open it.

He shoved away from the shore, climbing in and reaching for the paddle, letting the canoe drift for a moment until he had oriented himself. Paddling quietly, hardly disturbing the water with his careful strokes, Grady headed downstream, his mind on the woman who had freed them, a prayer raised for her, that she would find her freedom but more importantly, find her way to God.

Grady paused for a moment in a quiet spot in the stream, his paddle resting across his knees, his eyes on Eineen as she slept. He was worried about her and knew he had to get her to help, but just how he could do that, he had no idea. He was unfamiliar with this area and he wasn't even sure if he was anywhere near Eineen's home or that of her parents. He prayed for her family, knowing that they would be beside themselves with not knowing where she was.

He pulled out the piece of paper that he had been handed, twisting it until he could read the bold black lettering. He didn't recognize the name. Silas Peters. He frowned, his eyes raising. Or did he? The name seemed familiar, but he just didn't think he could place him.

Dipping his paddle into the water once more, he thrust with strong strokes that belied the fatigue hitting at him in waves, determined to reach the town that he could see up ahead through the rising mist of the early morning. He reached a dock and stopped, his head bowing for a moment as he offered a prayer of thankfulness and then one of deep begging almost, pleading for help.

Chapter 6

Rousing as Grady shook her gently, Eineen blinked rapidly, not sure where she was other than she was not in that cabin that she had begun to detest. She sat up, Grady's hand ready to help her from the canoe, before he reached back into it for their packs.

"Grady? Where are we?

How did we get here?"

"By canoe, along a stream in the moonlight, which you slept through." Grady grinned at the outraged look that came over her face before he sobered. "Mac's wife got us out, led me to the canoe, and sent us on our way. I worry about her."

Eineen snorted. "She likely knew what she was getting into when she went there to live. Although that does not excuse him." She turned in a circle. "What town is this? Why are we here?"

Grady reached for her hand, leading her rapidly through the marina and to an all-night cafe, shoving her into a seat in a booth once they were inside, dropping down beside her, their packs on the opposite side. He ignored the pointed looks that she darted his way.

Lord, I have no idea what I do now. Mac's wife sent us here, sent us to see Silas Peters, only I have no way of knowing how to reach him or if this is even the town that we would find him in.

Grady looked up and nodded at the coffee pot the waitress was holding up, glancing at Eineen as she shook her head

"Eineen, what would you like?"

"Just some milk and rye toast, please." She laid her head on his shoulder, fatigue still weighing her down, that and the lack of proper nutrition over the past week, to say nothing of the tumble they had taken, with injuries that she had not been able to have addressed.

Grady sipped at his coffee, his eyes searching for anyone who seemed interested in them. No one, he thought, is that interested, other than that of townspeople with strangers. He frowned as the door opened and two men entered. One has to be a cop, he thought, before his attention centred on the other one. I should know him, he thought. He frowned again, feeling Eineen shifting closer to him, as the two men approached their booth, hesitated for a moment before the one he had thought to be a police officer pointed to the bench seat.

"May we join you?"

Grady shrugged, not saying anything, waiting as the men sat, placed their orders, exchanged a glance and then focused on the couple across from them.

"You were right, Andrew. Sam said they'd head this way."

"I was, wasn't I, Silas? I have no idea how he knew that they would." The man called Andrew reached over to shake their hands. "I'm Andrew McBeth, police chief of this town. Sam Douglas got word to me. He was approached and told that you two would be heading this way."

Grady shrugged, not quite sure of them, before he ducked his head to watch Eineen, finding her with her eyes down, not looking at the men, but he could see the tenseness in her face.

"I'm Grady. And this is Eineen." Grady bit into his piece of toast, taking the time to try and come up with a plan, or something, he thought, that would get them out of there and to safety. He wasn't sure that the police chief was who he said he was.

Andrew grinned, reaching for his identification and sliding it across the table, directed at Eineen, who stared at it, not reacting at all. Andrew shared a puzzled look with Silas before Silas spoke.

"Grady, I'm Silas Peters, a minister in this town. I was approached late last night by someone, who will not be named, stating that you two were being sent to me. The request was that I help you out."

Grady nodded. "We were told to find you. I wasn't even sure if this was the right town." He reached for Eineen's hand. "We'll talk, Eineen. We will talk, that I promise you. I'll get you back to your parents and Eames."

"Eames? Who's that?" Eineen stared up at him, puzzled at his words.

"He's my friend, and your brother, older than you by about eighteen months. It will come back." Grady caught a glimpse of the look the two men across from him had shared. "Can we leave now? I don't feel safe out here. If someone has gotten word to you to expect us, then someone else may be looking for us."

"That's our fear, Grady. Eineen." Andrew rose, reaching for the packs he had moved to the floor when they had taken their seats. "Head towards the kitchen. We'll leave through there."

With her hand tight in Grady's, Eineen walked as close to him as she could get, her eyes on what she could see of his face. She didn't feel safe but had no idea why she didn't.

That scared her.

Grady could feel the tension in Eineen from the tight way she gripped his hand, hers shaking with what he assumed to be fear. He prayed for her, wishing it didn't have to be this way, that he could take her directly home, but he knew better. Not until he had talked to her, told her what Mac's wife had requested that he do, and then and only then would he contact her father, once they had resolved what to do. He shook his head mentally. How could he ask that of her? He could not ask her to marry him, not without being in love. That just wasn't done, not in this day and age. People simply did not marry one another to protect them.

Chapter 7

Staring at his host and then at his hostess, Grady's mouth opened and closed, but he could not form any words to speak. He shot a glance at Andrew, seeing a grin on his face at his reaction.

Eineen stared as well, not sure what the issue was. This couple seemed happy and in love. She had missed what had been said, her mind trying to comprehend just how much danger she was in, and trying to determine just who she was anyway.

Grady was finally able to sputter out some words, what they had been, he would not have been able to tell afterward.

"It's true, Grady. Silas and I married to protect one another. We had an adventure that we will tell you at some point. But when we married, I wasn't able to speak, just from the trauma of what we had faced. At least you two didn't find a dead body in the church."

"A what?" Grady's face paled as he stuttered out his words. "Did you say a dead body?"

"That's right. That started off our adventure." Silas grinned down at his wife. "But we were in love, I had been in love with her for a long time, just didn't know how to approach her." His glance turned to Andrew and his grin widened. "Now, Andrew here. He went in undercover to a roadhouse and rescued the lady who became his wife. She too wasn't able to speak.

She had been held hostage for a while. They are very much in love, before you ask."

Silas suddenly sat forward, sobering, a question on his face. "You were sent here for a reason, I think, Grady."

Grady nodded, his eyes on Eineen, finding her staring at Madigan Peters, a frown on her face.

"I know you." Eineen's voice was soft.

"You do, Eineen. But I'm not sure you remember from where." Madigan was on her feet, her hand reaching for Eineen, drawing her up to her own feet before she linked an arm with Eineen and walked her from the room. "You need to clean up. I have some clothes for you."

Eineen stopped in the bedroom that she had been shown to, looking around the tastefully decorated room. "This is too nice for me."

"Eineen?" When Madigan had her attention, she continued. "I have seen your parents' home and your cabin. We are friends. Your place is just as nice or nicer." Madigan's head tilted before she reached to hug Eineen.

"I don't remember. I don't remember anything." Eineen blinked back the tears that she refused to shed.

Madigan's soft voice soothed Eineen's anxiety as she prayed for her before stepping back and pointing to the bathroom.

"I can only imagine that you need to clean up. Go ahead. Come down when you're done or else have a nap."

Eineen nodded, turning her head to watch the door close behind Madigan, before she moved to pick up the pile of clothes on the bed and head for a much-needed shower. Refreshed, she stood staring at the bed before resolutely heading for the door, opening it to find Grady leaning on the wall, his eyes locked on her door, reaching to draw her into a tight hug, her own arms coming around him.

"Grady? What do we do?"

"We talk, first. Silas has a really nice backyard. How be we find one of the benches and sit for a bit?" Grady turned her and walked her down the stairs, an arm around her, reaching to grab two water bottles on the way through the kitchen, a nod at Madigan as she stood watching. He frowned at the sight of another woman waiting before his attention went back to Eineen.

He seated her on a love seat near the back of the yard, handing her an opened water bottle, watching as she sipped. He sighed. This is not going to be easy, is it, Lord? How do I do this?

Eineen watched Grady out of the corner of her eye, her heart raised in prayer to a God she somehow knew she loved and served but couldn't quite remember. She also knew that whatever it was that Grady wanted to talk to her about would dramatically change their friendship and her life.

Finally, unable to wait for him to speak, she turned to face him, her mouth opening, only to not speak as his finger was laid across her lips. His look was compassionate but there was something else in it, something she just couldn't read, but what gave her hope that she really did have a defender in her corner.

"Eineen, I was so afraid all week for you. I wanted so badly to get you away but I just didn't know how to. We weren't allowed any freedom." Grady's gaze dropped, not sure how to continue.

"They wouldn't have let me go, would they?" Eineen's voice held conviction of that fact, even though it held sadness as well. "He would have just given me to one of them."

Grady nodded, his eyes on the ground, watching as ants moved around an anthill not too far from his feet. Lord, You made these industrious little creatures. You care for them, but You care so much for us. You show us mercies in so many ways. Your compassion is so encompassing. Your faithfulness is so great.

"That was the plan. That's why Mac's wife got us out last night. She didn't have to say. Today, that would have been the day that it happened. Of that, I am convinced. She put her own life on the line to do that."

"The poor thing. How can we help her?" Eineen's thoughts flew to the older woman, having seen kindness hidden deep within her.

"We'll figure out some way. I just don't know if I will remember where they were, or if they'd even be there now. But, when we go back home, we'll put in a complaint to the police, and let them deal with them."

—

"Andrew?" Eineen's voice held a question.

"Andrew? What about him?"

"Can't he talk to them? He can take our statements, can't he?"

"He can. So, we need to be careful about what we say to each other or someone else." He looked up as he sensed a presence coming towards them and stood.

Bill Buckley, a detective on the force, stood for a moment before he nodded. You're right, Andrew. He's in over his head in love with her but doesn't know what to do.

"I'm Bill Buckley, a detective with the force. Andrew asked that I come and speak with you, get your statements, and then see what we can do about contacting the force in your town." Bill dropped down into a seat across from them. "So, who goes first?" His grin lit up his face as they stared at him and then one another.

"Eineen can go first." Grady went to stand again, to leave, but Eineen's quick clutching at his arm kept him in place. "Can I stay or do I need to leave?"

Bill shrugged. "You can stay. Let me get what Eineen has to say and then we'll get your statement."

Chapter 8

Bill finally stood to leave, his eyes on the couple in front of him, before they raised to stare past them. *This is a difficult one, Lord. How do we proceed? We can't let anyone know where they are. Eineen will disappear and Grady would be dead, killed trying to protect her.*

"I can't stress enough, you two, that you stay safe. For now, stay with Silas and Madigan. They have an apartment in the basement that you can use." Bill walked away, stopping by Silas, who stood on his back deck.

"I thought you had a meeting this morning." Bill turned to watch Grady and Eineen.

"I did, but Paul took it on for me. He was glad to. Didn't even ask the reason."

"That's our church family, isn't it? Stepping in with no questions asked." Bill nodded down the yard. "What's your reading on them?"

"Grady is determined to keep her safe at all costs. The note I got? It suggested quite sternly that I marry them. Eineen? She's terrified of being found again but trusting completely in Grady. It's unfortunate that she doesn't remember what happened or who she is."

"Walter heading out here to assess them?" Bill referred to a physician friend from church.

—

47

"He is. In fact, he's coming for supper. He didn't seem to think that it would matter at this point if he waited until then."

Bill nodded. "Okay. Have him talk to me. With their permission, of course." He walked away, his mind already racing as to how he could approach the police force in Mapleview, without giving away where the couple was.

Grady's hand reached for Eineen's, clasping hers tightly before he hesitated and then spoke.

"Mac's wife asked something else of me, Eineen, but I'm not sure it's the right way for us to proceed."

"And that would be?" Eineen was puzzled.

"She told me to marry you and to do it today." Grady refused to look at Eineen, not wanting to see the rejection in her face. When there was a silence that continued, he twisted on the bench, his eyes finding hers on him. "Eineen?"

Eineen wet her lips with her tongue, hesitating to speak but knowing that she had to. "Grady? Is that what you want?" She waited as he paused before he nodded. She sighed. "That's what I thought you would say. It's not fair to you."

"Nor to you, Eineen. You need to be wooed and courted and have your parents and brother to be part of this"

She nodded in turn. "I know. It's not fair to you. Your parents? You have parents, don't you?"

—

He laughed before he nodded. "I do. They're out in Alberta right at the moment, at a camp out there. Dad was asked to speak at a conference."

"Your Dad? What does he do?"

"He's a minister. Mom has always been able to go with him when he speaks at conferences. They have a mission set up, where they go in and speak at workplaces. My sisters are involved in mission work as well, one in Toronto at a mission for the homeless. That's my older sister. The younger one? She works at a church in our hometown."

"I didn't know that." Eineen sighed. "How would they take something like this?"

"As long as we have prayed it through, feel the peace that God is directing our steps, they'd be okay. Disappointed not to be here, but they would be fine. They know of you, Eineen, because of your brother, Eames."

Eineen nodded, her eyes raising to study the sky through the colouring leaves. Early fall, she thought, my favourite time of year and when I always wished to be married. But not like this. Not to someone that I really don't know but who I know cares what happens to me and wants to protect me. He tells me I have parents and a brother. Right now, I need them, and I don't remember them and don't want to be around them. They would not be safe. Dear Lord, what do I do? Do I take this offer for safety, just as Ruth did when she wed Boaz? This is a different day and age, I know, Lord, but You are the same. You never change. Your compassions never fail. Your great faithfulness

—

encompasses us and protects us, only allowing what You will in our lives. What do I do, Lord?

Grady waited, his eyes on Eineen's face before he muttered something low enough that she could not hear or understand and simply sweep her into a hug, his arms tight around her, promising his protection and strength. Her head rested against the left side of his chest, hearing his strong steady heartbeat, and knowing that was his character. Her hand rested on his chest near her face, a fingernail flicking lightly at the dark blue button on the dark blue shirt he had been given to wear.

Eineen finally tilted her head enough so that she could study his face. He told her that her brother was friends with him, and given that, she had likely heard of him, but she really didn't know him, now did she? She waited for the Lord, finding a peace filling her heart, and knowing that the Lord had spoken to her in the still small voice she seemed to remember.

"I will, Grady. God help me, I will." Her voice was low, broken in tone somewhat, sorrow edging it, but a confidence in God and in him coming through.

"Okay. Then, I guess we do this." Grady paused, his eyes on her before he bent his head and gently kissed her. His forehead rested against hers before he spoke.

"Are you sure?"

Eineen nodded. "I think so."

She raised her head to study his face once more before she turned, sensing someone near them.

Silas and Madigan stood for a moment, before they sat in the bench across from them, the other woman Grady had seen taking a seat on the ground, her eyes on the late-season rose that she was holding.

"Grady, Eineen. This is Andrew's wife, Phoebe. He asked that she come and meet with you, to tell you their story, if it helps."

Eineen frowned. "Phoebe? Why do I know that name?"

Phoebe looked up, a gentle smile on her face. "We have met, Phoebe. At a young women's retreat a couple of years ago. I was a newlywed as was Madigan. It was held in your town, and you welcomed us to stay with you."

"You know me?" Eineen leaned forward. "Tell me. Do I really have parents and a brother?"

Phoebe began to laugh, Madigan joining her. "You do, Eineen. Indeed, you do. Your brother loves to tease you but he watches out for you all the time. We saw that. Your parents are a lovely committed Christian couple, who really blessed us with their wisdom and wit."

"Okay." Eineen leaned back against Grady, his arm resting lightly around her. She looked up at him, seeing his smile. "I didn't doubt you. I am just so unsure of things."

"That you will be." Silas spoke, and then began to pray, a fervent pleading prayer for the couple in front of him. When he finished, he raised his head. "I sense that you two have made a decision."

Chapter 9

His eyes on Eineen, Grady finally nodded. "We have. We have decided to marry. I don't know of any other way to keep her safe. Even at that, I am not sure that it will be a success." He bit his lip as he raised his head to stare at Silas. "What I was told was that I had to get Eineen away and marry her right away, that the monster who had held us had planned to give her to one of his men, and that it would have been today."

Silas nodded, even as he heard the exclamations from Madigan and Phoebe. "That does change things." He looked over at Phoebe. "When Phoebe was held captive, part of the reason was that she was to be given to someone, and not with marriage in mind. God protected her. He will protect you two. I can't guarantee that you won't face danger."

"We realize that, Silas. How do we do this?"

"First, you and I need to get the license. Do you have your identification?" Silas prayed that they did. Otherwise, this would not work.

Eineen pulled out a slim wallet she had tucked down into her jeans pocket. "Here. This says it's me. I don't remember it. It has my birth certificate, and whatever else you would need."

Grady shifted to pull his wallet from his front jeans pocket.

"And I have mine. Where do we go?"

Silas stood, a grin on his face. "If you can let Eineen go for a bit, then you and I will head to the downtown area. I know the clerk in the city hall we have to see. She's the pianist at our church." He turned to Eineen. "Madigan and Phoebe will help you. Madigan has some plans, thinking this might be what is facing you. Trust her, Eineen, if you can."

Eineen watched the men walk away, fear in her that she had to tamp down, fear that whoever it was would find Grady and harm him. She turned as she felt arms around her and both Madigan and Phoebe sitting beside her, the ladies praying for her, before Madigan rose, drawing her to her feet once more. The ladies linked arms with her, heading for the house.

"I know it's difficult, Eineen." Madigan shared a look with Phoebe. "Both Phoebe and I married quickly, without our family with us, just for protection. Now, I think we're of a size. I have a wedding dress that was my mother's. We can use it. I never got to, but I know she would be honoured to have you use it."

An hour later, Eineen stood, staring at herself in the full-length mirror, wonder and awe on her face.

"This is me?" She spun to face the two ladies.

"It is you. It fits you almost perfectly. Now, do you want the veil, or just leave your beautiful hair loose?" Phoebe reached to touch a strand.

Silas stood just inside the door to the local jewelry shop, listening to Grady's quiet conversation with the clerk about wedding bands and then heard him ask for the engagement rings, he needed one for his lady. He nodded. God, You are here with them. He is

---

in love with her, that I can see. Protect them. His attention was drawn to the hulking unkempt man pacing along the sidewalk on the other side of the street, stopping to peer through the windows. He moved back. He knew that man and knew that he was looking for only two people.

"Grady? Are you about done?" He moved to stand beside Grady.

Grady looked up, a frown flittering across his face before he nodded. "I am. Trouble?"

"There is. Sarah, can we leave through the back door?"

Sarah looked up, seeing the warning on Silas' face. "You can. Just follow me." Sarah moved away from them to lock the turn and turn the sign to closed. "We can just lock up for a bit. It's almost lunchtime. Besides, you need a pianist, don't you, Silas?" Her grin had him laughing.

"We do if Grady is in agreement."

"I am in full agreement of anything that makes this day special for my lady." He paused, dismay on his face. "I don't have a suit. Or flowers." When Silas began to laugh, he turned to glare at him. "I don't see that this is funny."

Silas continued to grin as he tried to control his laughter. "At least, you'll have a suit. I can lend you one. Our garden is full of flowers, thanks to my wife's green thumb. I would suspect she is already surveying the flowers, picking out a selection for you to choose from of her very best. You have your rings. And a minister. And a pianist. I would also suspect that Madi has pulled out her Mom's wedding dress for Eineen. She never got to wear it herself, we were married so quickly and in Riverville by a friend of mine. What more do you need?"

Grady shrugged before he grinned. "Nothing. I just wish it was different." He sobered at the thought.

"Andrew said he would be back this afternoon. He has Bill calling someone in your town, a Sam Douglas, I think he said, who had called him."

"Sam? Sure. He's a friend of Eineen's father." Grady groaned. "Now, how do we do this?"

"With God, my friend. With God's help." Silas peeked out the back door of the shop, before pointing to the parking lot. "Let's move. Sarah, we'll see you at our house."

Chapter 10

Two hours later, Grady stood, watching Eineen as she moved quietly around the small suite in Silas' basement, the white dress that she still wore whispering softly around her. She was avoiding him, he knew, and just shook his head, loosening his tie and pulling it off to drop on the table. Silas had told him that Andrew had had some friends shop for them and had left the packages in the bedroom.

He walked through the suite, noting the warm colours that belied it being below grade level, the larger windows letting in much light before he paused at the bedroom door, surprised at the number of packages waiting for him. He reached for them, sorting through what would be his, and then stood, his head turned to listen for Eineen, hearing soft muttering coming from her, a smile creasing his face.

Grady changed rapidly, the suit and tie set to one side, before he stood, staring down at the debris he had left on the bed before he sighed, tidying it away, leaving the clothes for Eineen piled neatly on the dresser, his own going into the brand new duffle bag waiting for him.

Eineen appeared at that point, surprise on her own face as he pointed to the clothing.

"This is for me? Who?"

"Andrew. He said he had some friends shop for us. He's refusing to take anything for it."

"Oh, my. This is nice, but I have no idea if these are the colours and styles that I like."

"They will be. The ladies would have talked to Madigan and Phoebe, more than likely. I know Andrew picked my brain as to my choices."

Grady's hand on her arm stopped her for a moment. "I'm sorry it had to be this way, Eineen, but I am not sorry that it's you. You are God's choice for me. Always have been." He turned and walked away, a low whistle of a favourite hymn trailing him, and she soon heard the water running in the kitchen and then the odour of a freshly-opened package of coffee.

Eineen changed quickly, not really caring what she wore, the wedding dress carefully folded and the shoes placed with it, ready to return to Madigan. She hesitated, a brief vision stopping her of an older lady hugging her when she was young. Who is that, Lord?

Hearing a tap at the door, she moved towards the living room, finding Grady greeting Silas. She spun, heading back to gather their borrowed clothing, her hand resting for a moment on the suit Grady had worn. Phoebe had willingly taken pictures of them, Andrew standing beside Grady even as Madigan had stood beside her. She wiped a tear from her cheek, sadness welling in her for what reason she could not say.

Grady watched as Eineen padded towards him, a hand reaching for hers, even as Silas reached for the bundle she had in her arms.

"Madigan has asked if you would join us for supper. We have a friend, a physician, who has agreed to stop by, just to make sure that you two are okay. Bill has also asked if he can drop by. He needs to speak with you two again." Silas paused before he continued. "I'm sorry."

"Sorry. Why?" Eineen stared up at him.

"This is not how you two should have celebrated today. You need good memories. We have to bring in others that aren't."

Eineen shrugged. "I don't think we can help it, now can we?" She brushed past Silas, who caught the glimmer of tears in her eyes.

Grady hesitated before he walked forward, a grim look on his face. "What does Bill have to say, did Andrew indicate anything?"

"No, he didn't. He wouldn't, not when it's you two that they need to speak with. Just now that you are being prayed for. We have asked our friends to pray, giving only your names and that you need it."

"Thank you." Grady pulled out Eineen's phone. "I have her phone. But she doesn't remember the password. I wish she did. I'm sure her parents and Eames have been trying to reach her."

"I am sure they have. If anything, let Bill have it. The techs might be able to unlock it for you."

"That's a thought. I'll run it by her."

Grady stood for a moment, watching as Eineen spoke with Madigan and Phoebe, his heart wondering that God had chosen him for her and her for him before he looked around, a frown on his face as he saw someone he didn't know

———

"Grady? This is Walter, a friend from church. He is also a physician. He would like to examine you two, just to be on the safe side." Andrew had approached.

"No problem. Listen, did you say Bill was coming around?"

"He is. He and his wife, Cora, and his little guy." Andrew watched Grady's face closely. "I hope we haven't overstepped."

"No, that's fine. I really need for Eineen to be looked at. I'm afraid to take her to a clinic or the hospital. He would likely be watching those."

"He would. Silas didn't tell you that he saw him today when you were in the jewelry store."

"That explains why he had us leave by the back doorway. Smart thinking."

His young son in his arm, Bill stood for a moment, his other arm around Cora, before he spoke.

"That's Grady and Eineen. Silas married them today. They're having an adventure."

"Oh, I pray that it is nothing like ours. I came too close to losing you." Cora moved forward, leaving Bill to head towards Grady.

Grady spun as he heard Bill's voice and then smiled at Bill's son.

"Who do we have here?"

"My son. Aaron. How are you now?"

Grady shrugged. "Not sure about anything anymore. Just one question, before we eat. Did you talk to anyone in the force at home?"

"I did. Sam Douglas. I've worked with him many times."

"Good. He knows Eineen. In fact, he and his wife are good friends of her parents."

"That's what he said. Now, Aaron, down you go. I think Madigan's kitten is around somewhere. Just don't pull its tail again."

Aaron grinned up at his father, nodding. "Tail. Pull. Kitten. I find."

Bill groaned. "And he will do just that. I should have kept my mouth shut."

Grady's laughter spilled over, causing Eineen to turn towards him, taking the hand he had reached out for her.

"Bill?" She was hesitant as she said his name.

Bill merely grinned. "I told my son not to pull the kitten's tail. He is now on a mission to do just that."

Chapter 11

Earlier that day, Bill had sunk into his chair in his office, exhausted, even though it was only early afternoon. He listened to his voice mail messages, sorted through them, and then studied the pile of folders on his desk. He sighed. He needed to be out early tonight and he just wasn't sure he would make it.

Studying the top message, Bill finally reached for the phone. When he made this call, it would likely change things for his new friends as he thought of them. Grady and Eineen were in danger, of that he had no doubt. Marrying as they had? If their captor ever got his hands on them, Grady's life would be worthless and who knows what he would do to Eineen.

"Morgan." Sam's voice was abrupt, deep as he was in the reports on his desk.

"Sam Morgan? It's Bill Buckley." Bill could hear the silence for a moment and then the creak of a desk chair as Sam settled back.

"Bill Buckley. I haven't talked to you in a while, in what eight, ten months?"

"Something like that. How's your family?"

"They're good. Girls are through college now and working. How's Cora?"

"She's good, busy. I don't know if you had heard but we have a little guy, eight months old now."

"I had heard rumours. Congratulations." They spoke for a few minutes on general items before Sam hesitated. "You called for a reason, did you not, Bill?"

"I did. Your request for someone to watch for a certain couple landed on my desk."

"And?" Sam sat forward, reaching for a pad of paper and his pen. "You have news?"

"I do, Sam. Good news. We have them. Andrew and Silas found them in a cafe near the marina. They had arrived in town in a canoe."

"A canoe, you say? That means they came from upstream. Did Grady say where?"

"He's not sure. It wasn't an area he was familiar with, but he did say it was dark when they set out, he thought somewhere around eleven at night or later. They landed in town in the early morning, around six or so, Andrew said."

"So that means?" Sam did some rapid calculations and then reached for a map. Bill could hear the rustle as he unfolded it. "I can see an area likely close to where they started from. It's one we've had under surveillance. Now, wouldn't it be nice if we could just walk in and take these guys!"

"I doubt you will. Grady said it was Mac's wife who got them out."

"His wife? She's got some backbone at last."

"You know her?"

"I've seen her around. Very beaten down, but there is a spark in her eyes that says she's just waiting for her time to walk away. What else can you tell me?"

"She told Grady that Mac planned to give Eineen to one of his men, likely the next day. She couldn't or wouldn't allow that. Grady seems okay, but we have a problem with Eineen."

"We do? What would that be?"

Bill hesitated once more, before he prayed, asking for the right words. "She doesn't remember who she is. She doesn't remember her parents. She doesn't remember her brother. Not one thing about them."

"Then she was hurt in the tumble down the slope. We were afraid of that." Sam sat in silence, digesting what he had been told.

"I'll need to talk to her parents and brother. When can they see her?"

"Right at the moment? I would suggest that they wait. They are more than likely to be watched. Grady got the impression that Eineen was taken for revenge or to force her father to do something."

"That's what we're hearing on the streets. This won't go over well. They will want to be there. They will not want her on her own, even with Grady there."

"Yeah, about Grady." Bill shook his head. How did he say it?

"Bill? What aren't you saying?"

"About Grady. Mac's wife had one request of him."

Sam groaned. "Don't tell me."

"That he marry her."

"I told you not to tell me that. How do I explain that to her parents?" Sam was frustrated, to say the least.

"That Grady stepped in, doing the only thing he could think of to keep her safe. And before you ask, between us? He's head over heels for her. He'll do everything he can."

"I know he will." Sam pondered that for a moment before he sighed. "And knowing Grady, he will have prayed it through thoroughly."

"The same with Silas when the request was made. You know Silas and Madigan's story and that of Andrew and Phoebe. They shared part of their stories with this couple, helping them to see it was not all lost."

The pair spoke for a few more minutes, trying to make plans for eventualities that they were not even certain would come to fruition. Sam sighed as he placed his phone on his desk, his head bowing for a moment, raising it as he heard a tap at the door, beckoning in his supervisor.

"Sam? You look relieved but worried. Care to share?"

Sam did just that, surprise colouring the other officer's face.

—

"I'm heading out to talk to them. I don't like that it's under these circumstances."

"A word of advice, Sam? Go after work. Go as a friend, not an officer. I'll back you in this." His supervisor rose. "I'll call Andrew and see what his feelings are about this. I don't like that Mac that is the one we're looking for. He will not rest until he has them in his hands again."

"That's what worries me. That's why Bill has said for her parents not to approach them. And I just don't know how I can stop them."

"It will be difficult, I grant you that. God will go ahead of you. Of that, I am confident."

Chapter 12

Driving up the long lane that led to Garrett's home, Sam stopped his truck, put it in park, and bowed his head. He needed to pray, he thought. God, this is when You need to show Your merciful character and Your compassion. I can't do that for You. I can sympathize with them, but it's not my little girl. I can't take that burden from them. That only You can do and only if they give it to You.

Sam finally pulled to a stop outside Garrett's home, a sigh going through him. Eames was there, and he knew it would be difficult to stop him from heading out. He would have to watch his words, not name the town or the people involved. And that would be difficult. Lord, put a watch on my tongue, please?

Garrett stood on the front porch, a frown on his face as he watched Sam walk towards him. His steps are heavy, Lord. I don't like that. He began to prepare his mind and heart for the news his little girl was dead.

"Sam? What brings you out here tonight?"

Sam paused his steps at the bottom of the few steps, his eyes on Garrett before moving to the doorway where Esther, Garrett's wife, stood, Eames' arm around her.

"I need to talk with you three. Part as an officer, part as a friend."

Garrett's eyes slid closed. "She's gone, isn't she?"

Sam shook his head, walking up the steps, a hand to his friend's shoulder. "No, she's alive. But I do need to talk with you three. Inside would be better. Someone is watching your place. We've seen evidence of that."

Garrett moved backward, feeling Esther's hand on his back before he stopped.

"I see. Come on in, Sam. Good of you to drop by. Esther has some fresh peach pie I think you'll enjoy. We were just about to have our dessert. Good timing."

"Thanks, Garrett. I've been wanting a piece of her peach pie. Esther, thank you. Eames, what have you been up to?" Sam pointed to the ceiling of the porch, Garrett nodding, a surprised look on his face.

Once inside, Garrett moved to close the windows, Eames doing the same, before they were seated in the kitchen.

"What was that about, Sam?" Garrett handed over a plate with the pie on it.

"You have monitoring devices out there. They didn't hide them too well."

"So, then, everything we've said has been heard?"

"Could be. I don't remember seeing them there yesterday."

"That would have been what I heard last night." Esther's face grew sober, a frightened look to it.

"It likely was, love. I looked but didn't see anything. I didn't think to look at the ceiling." Garrett watched Sam closely. "Sam, I think we need to spend some time in prayer. I fear for what you have to tell us."

Sam finally raised his head, studying his friends, seeing the hope in their face and their eyes, struggling to find the words to tell them what he had been told.

"Sam? Is Eineen alive?" Eames could barely ask the question, not knowing his father already had.

"She is, Eames, and for now, she's safe. She's hidden in another town."

"Can we see her?" This from the mother, who was just so desperate to see her daughter and hold her, to try and make it all better for her.

"No, not at the moment." He lifted his hand at their protest. "It's at the request of the other town's force that we are taking this step. Eineen's life is in grave danger and so is Grady's."

"They're together?" Garrett's voice asked the question they had all wondered about.

Sam gave a snort of laughter, startling the three.

"Sam? What did I say that was so funny?" Garrett was puzzled.

"They're together. Let me tell you what I can. Grady has stated that the bank behind the caves gave way and they tumbled down it. He awoke early the next morning and not long after he roused, three men found them and took them captive once more. They were walked a number of hours from there. He carried Eineen as she had not roused.

"Once they were at a sheltered encampment, Grady says they were shoved into a small cabin, questioned and threatened a number of times in a day for a week. Finally, last night, a woman in the encampment freed them, took them to a canoe, and sent them on their way. He paddled all night until he reached a town, made contact with the police there, who put them into protection."

Garrett's face had gone through many changes as Sam had spoken, sure that he had not said everything.

"What aren't you telling us, Sam?" Eames spoke, his eyes on his father.

Sam's lips narrowed, as he could feel anger building up in him. Lord, I need to let it go and on my own, I can't. How do I tell them?

"What I am about to tell you, goes no further." He searched the three faces in front of him.

"If Eineen had not been removed from that camp last night, she would never have been allowed to leave. Grady more than likely would have been killed trying to protect her. We know who had her. And no, I will not say who. It's part of the investigation. His plan was to keep her in his camp, giving her to one of his men." Sam heard the sharp in-drawing of Esther's breath and then soft sobs from her, watching as Garrett's arms went around her, one hand reaching to touch his son.

———

"He would have done that?"

Sam nodded. "It's not the first time that we have heard rumours of that. Grady wouldn't have made it. I know him. He would have done his best to prevent it. They are still not safe. This man will seek revenge against her, for thwarting all of his plans."

"But now what?" Eames spoke for the three of them.

Sam gave a grim smile. "Grady was told to do something, something that may be the only way to keep Eineen alive. Even at that, we are not sure that it will." He paused, taking a sip of his coffee, to steady himself and get his emotions under control. "Grady and Eineen were married today, both in agreement that it was probably the only step they could take. Grady did not like it that you could not be part of it."

"Can we at least talk with her?" Esther's heart was breaking at what she had been told.

"I can see if I can arrange it at some point over the next few days. But there is something else you need to be aware of. Eineen has no memory of you three, or of any part of her life prior to waking up in the camp. She must have taken a blow to her head when they fell, and that in a combination of some deep fear she has been dealing with, that had taken her memories away. Grady is the only one she will open up to. That much I have been told."

Chapter 13

Garrett wandered his home late that night, knowing that Esther had retired, but not likely to sleep. She had been devastated, as had he and Eames, by what Sam had told them. He had a suspicion of who was involved but would say nothing, knowing that Eames might well head out to find the man, and end up dead.

Eames stood for a moment, his eyes on the mantle, staring at the enlarged photo on it of the four of them. Lord, I don't understand. I don't know what to think, what to say. He moved towards his father, stopping by the desk in the living room, his finger rubbing along the edge of it.

"Dad? What do we do?"

Garrett sighed, having asked himself that question many times. "I have no idea, Eames. I really don't know. We have to respect the wishes of the police force in whatever town they are in, leaving it to their discretion to contact us when they feel it is safe. We can get word to them through Sam, at least, I think we can."

"Sam told me that. He suggested we write letters, find some photos, whatever it might take to trigger Eineen's memories." Eames blinked rapidly, unable to control the tears that flooded his eyes, feeling his father's arms around him, just as he had when a small boy and needing comfort. He clung to him, their

---

faces wet with their tears before he heard Garrett begin to pray.

Eames finally moved away, wandering the room just as his father had. He finally stopped, turning to find his father watching him

"Dad, do you know who it might be?"

"Not really. I have some ideas, and no, I will not tell you." Garrett sighed. "I know that you want to find your sister and find the man or men responsible. We can't do that, son. No matter how much we want to. We have to wait for the authorities. I am sure they will interview Eineen and Grady many times, and search where they might have been. I am not sure that we would even know where to begin."

Eames drew a deep breath. "That's what I don't get, Dad. Why Eineen? Who is her enemy?"

"That I don't know. I know she's been hiding something. We've all seen it. What it is, I have no idea. She wouldn't talk about it."

"So you think it might have something to do with what she's just gone through?"

"It's possible. I didn't feel comfortable with her wandering around on her on the last month or so, but I had no facts to tell her, and she wouldn't have quit just for suspicions."

"No, she wouldn't have. It scares me, Dad, knowing she's like she is, and we can't go help her."

"It scares me, too, as it does your mother." Garrett squinted at the clock. "It's too late for you to

—

72

head home, son. Head up to your old room. Mom has it ready for you.”

“Thanks, Dad. I don't know that I'll sleep much.” Eames' footsteps faded away, the weight of his worry sounding in them.

Garrett sighed as he reached to turn out lights, standing for a moment at the front door, a hand resting on the knob, staring out, not wanting to see anyone, but just wishing it was his daughter he saw, running towards him as she had as a younger girl. Lord, it hurts to hear what was planned. It hurts to hear that she has started a new life without our involvement. That is a hurt You will need to heal. We need to be covered with Your mercies and Your compassion at this time. Heal my girl, Lord. Bless this young man who stepped in, with no thought of his own life or safety, to take a step that no young man should be called upon to take in these days.

Garrett turned, his footsteps slow and aged as he headed for the hallway and then the bedroom, sinking down on it, kicking off his shoes and then laying beside his wife, gathering her to his heart, hearing her soft sobs and letting his own tears wet her hair.

—

Chapter 14

A week later, Eineen rose from the bench she had been sitting on at the back of the yard, her mind not on the scenery, but on why she could not remember who she was. She was beginning to get flashes of people and events and objects but so far, nothing made sense. That frightened her. Grady had worked with her, had held her when she sobbed in fear and frustration, his prayers bringing comfort as did his kisses that she felt on the top of her head. She had to admit it. She was falling in love with her husband and knew from his actions and his words that he loved her, but he would not push her to admit her feelings. He would just grin at her when she grumped at him about that and sweep her into a tight hug.

Walking towards her, his bare feet sinking into the grass, Grady studied Eineen before he looked down at the large envelope he held. Bill had been around, staying only long enough to drop it off. Grady had asked that he contact his employer. Bill had grinned, said they had already, and that Jim understood and wanted him to stay safe, even if it meant staying away. Grady had only been able to stammer out words of thanks before Bill had waved and drove away.

Eineen looked up, a smile coming to her face, and she almost ran towards Grady, finding him standing with arms open to welcome her.

They stood for a moment before she leaned back.

"You weren't supposed to be here. I thought you were meeting with Andrew."

"I was supposed to, but he's been called out of town.

Bill stopped by. You had a package delivered to him from Sam Douglas."

He watched as she frowned.

"Do I know him?"

"You do, my love. He's a good friend of your parents, but he is also a police officer in our hometown. Bill said the package was from your family."

Eineen froze for a moment, a frown wrinkling her brow.

"I guess I have to open it, don't I?"

"You really should. You do need to remember who you are. I would like that for you, my love." Grady had handed her the envelope as he spoke.

Eineen's fingers toyed with the sealed flap, her mind not on that, but on what Grady had called her. She tilted her head to study him.

"Am I that, Grady?"

"Are you what?" Grady was somewhat distracted until he looked at her face, and saw the yearning on it.

"You called me your love. Twice. Am I that?"

"You are, Eineen. I think you have been for a long time. I just didn't know it."

She sighed, leaning back into his hug, her arms around him.

"Thank you. I needed to hear that, to have that reassurance. To know I am important to someone I remember right now." She stepped back, her eyes on the envelope. "I think when I open this, it will change everything, won't it?"

"It will, but hopefully and I pray that it does, it will help you remember. Your parents and brother must be so sick with worry about you. I would be."

Grady's arm around her turned her towards the back deck.

Madigan had been out with a tray of sandwiches and drinks for them, waiting for them to approach.

"It's lunchtime, you two." She grinned as Eineen flushed.

"I let you do all the work again."

Madigan shrugged. "It's okay, Eineen. It's my turn to serve you. You did that with Phoebe and me, you know."

"But it wasn't for this long." Eineen sat, her hand reaching for Grady's as he prayed before she reached for a plate of salad. "I don't know if I liked salads before, but I enjoy yours. It must be the fresh veggies you gather from your garden."

Madigan shrugged, her eyes on the envelope, but not asking. It was not her place, she knew. She just prayed for her friends. When the meal was over, she went to rise, staying in place as Eineen looked up at her.

"Can you stay? I am not sure what I'm going to find. You know my parents and brother as well."

"I do, but not as well as Grady does."

"I really don't know her parents." Grady reached for the envelope, his hand laying flat on it. "I know her brother, Eames, better. We've been friends for a number of years."

Eineen finally opened the envelope, her fingers shaking as she slid them under the flap, and then raised the envelope to dump out the contents. She stared down at it, her shaking hands covering her mouth, even as Grady's arm came around her, bringing comfort, strength, and courage to her. She heard his prayer, even as she stared, not quite comprehending what all was there.

"Where do you start, my love?"

She shrugged. "I have no ideas. There are letters, photos, and what is that?" She pointed to an object, not quite sure of its origin.

Grady reached for it and then began to laugh, laughing hard enough he had to wipe his eyes.

"That would be Eames and his sense of humour. This, my love, appears to be a dried flower. You collect them, study them, write columns about them. In fact, you have become quite an expert in the flowers around our town."

"I have? I don't remember."

She sat silent, leafing through the photos, seeing herself with an older couple and then a younger man, not recognizing them. She set the letters aside, not quite ready to read what she gathered would be loving, intimate letters from her family, only she couldn't remember them.

Grady sensed her weariness and gathered everything but the letters back into the envelope. They were alone, Madigan having had to leave.

"Grady, what now? Do we go back there? I mean, I know we have to at some point."

"We do but for now, we can't. It's not safe. Andrew got word to me last night, and I need to talk to you, that your parents and brother are being watched and watched closely. We have come to the conclusion that Mac Duffy thinks that they know where you are. He will not cease looking for you until you are back in his hands. I couldn't take that, my love. Your parents can't either."

"Do they know?" Eineen's voice was quiet, unsure, worried. Grady couldn't put words to all the emotions she seemed to wrap in just those three words.

"They do. Bill talked to Sam, and he talked to your parents and your brother." He tapped the envelope. "This is why you have this. He arranged for it, at their request. They really want to talk to you, to hear your voice, but they understand that it is far too dangerous for you, and for them."

"For them? I don't understand." Eineen turned her gaze to him, seeing the worry he didn't hide from her.

"He will use them, if he has to, to get to you. Sam has done some digging on the quiet. The men who they think were the ones who originally took us work for Mac. It was another group that found us near the stream and took us to him. Sam also determined that you were taken as revenge against your father and to make him back away from the charges he was laying against Mac."

Chapter 15

Grady wandered the downtown area of Elmton, his intent to find something for his bride, but he just wasn't sure what. He paused in front of a store, not paying any attention to the passersby before he entered the store, searching through the books, finally picking one he thought Eineen would like. He looked up as he heard his name, surprised to find Silas beside him.

"Silas? You're here?"

"I am. Bill got word to me. Duffy is back in town, on a rampage, it seems, putting out word he wants you and Eineen, her alive, he really doesn't care in what condition you're in."

Grady paled. "I guess I shouldn't have come downtown. I just needed to get out of the house."

"We understand that, Grady. Just make sure one of us is with you, that's all Bill and Andrew are asking." Silas pointed to the back of the store. "Head that way. The owners won't say a word."

"You're sure?" Grady grabbed his package, a thank you to the clerk, and then followed Silas.

Silas came to an abrupt halt at the back door, his head tilting as he heard angry loud words outside it. He spun, searching, before with a hand to Grady's shoulder, he shoved him into an open room, the lunchroom for the store, shut the door and snicked the lock closed. He stood, ear to the door, Grady with a frown on his face before he spoke.

"What is this all about, Silas?"

"Your Mac Duffy? He was outside the back door. Someone called him by name."

Grady sank against the door, the back of his head resting against it as he looked up.

"He's found us. I blew it, didn't I?"

"Not necessarily." Silas held up a hand and then pointed to the door, mouthing that Duffy was outside there.

The two men waited, hearing the doorknob rattle and then the door shake violently as Duffy tried to enter. They also heard the quick tap of high heels as the older clerk appeared.

"You can't be back here. This is for employees only."

"I want in that room. Unlock it." Duffy's voice roared at her.

"I don't think so. This is a private area of the store. You need to leave and leave now."

"Not until I get in that room. I want to know who's hiding in there."

"Excuse me? You do not tell me what to do."

Silas could just picture Emily, the clerk, drawing herself up to her full five-foot stature and standing off against the hulking height that was Duffy. He knew

—

81

Duffy, had had trouble with him in the past, and wanted to do everything he could to avoid him.

The two men heard the sound of heavy boots tromping there way, and then the sharp commands of police officers. They also heard the struggle as Duffy resisted the men before they heard the sound of his body hitting the floor and then the faint snap of handcuffs around his wrists.

Silas and Grady waited, not wanting to leave too soon, but not wanting to put Emily at risk any longer. They finally heard a quiet tap at the door and then a second one.

Silas cracked the door open to see Bill standing with his back to him, his attention on the back door.

"Come on, you two. Out the back door and into the van I have here. I can't guarantee Duffy didn't have someone else out there."

"He did." Silas gave a grim smile. "Here, take these, Grady. Three should be enough to hide your face. Good thinking, Bill, to bring a van." Silas handed Grady some cartons of that were ready for the recycling but which had not been broken down as yet, grabbing some himself.

Bill grinned. "It was Emily's idea. She folded the flaps down on those boxes for you, suggested you take them. If you hadn't volunteered to take them, I was under her orders to hand them to you." Bill peeked out the door, and the motioned Grady and Silas out and into the van, cautioning them to stay low.

—

Grady caught a glimpse of a number of police officers milling around and frowned, his eyes on Silas as he grinned.

"Bill is part actor, I think. He would have arranged for extra officers to be here, to cover our escape." He turned to the front of the van, finding Andrew seated in the driver's seat, turned to watch them, a grin on his face, but a stern look around his eyes. "Home, James."

Andrew shook his head. "Not so fast. They'll expect us to take you there. I am not sure that we didn't totally cover your tracks back there. So for now, we make deliveries."

"Deliveries?" Grady stared around. "We only have these empty boxes."

"Exactly. Emily has set it up with some of the neighbouring merchants that I deliver one box to each one, and then head for the cafe outside of town. Someone will meet us there." Andrew began to laugh as he turned back to face the front of the van.

"I would think that she is enjoying herself."

"Oh, she is, Andrew. She is. I don't know if you're aware but she is quite a part of planning activities for the kids and teens. They all love it when it's her turn to come up with something."

"I wasn't aware of that. I have been remiss."

Chapter 16

Grady was on a hunt. He and Silas had returned home a short time ago, and he just needed to find his bride. Only she was nowhere to be found. That puzzled him and worried him. He turned back to the yard, heading for the bench that he knew she preferred, to come to a stop and to stand and stare at it. Eineen was just not around, at least, not where he felt comfortable looking.

He paced back towards the house, approaching it from the back patio, stepping up on the porch to move towards the door, pausing as he heard a sound. He spun and then was across the porch, on his knees beside Eineen, sweeping her to him before he rose and sat where she had been, cradling her close. He paid no attention to the papers scattering around him.

His sole concern was Eineen.

"Eineen?" He waited as the sobs ceased and she seemed to be gaining control of her emotions. "Eineen?"

"I read the letters, Grady. Oh, I should have waited for you. You need to read them." She looked up at him. "I read them, but it's like they're strangers. I don't know them. Will I ever remember?"

"Walter seemed to think you would. I have no reason to doubt him. You are starting to remember things."

"I know." She sounded grumpy and for once, Grady did not laugh at her or tease her. He just let her feel what emotions were bubbling to the top of the pile.

Grady waited, feeling Eineen beginning to relax, her weight resting against him. He stared down at the pages he could see before he looked up at her face.

"Eineen? What was in them that bothered you so much?"

"They talk as if they miss me, that they love me, that they want me to come home. I don't know them, Grady. I don't remember them. I look at their pictures and they're strangers. How do I go around them? They will expect me to be what they remember. Even if I do remember them, I'll never be that person again."

"No, you won't, and they won't expect you to. Sam has spoken with them in length, that I know. He has warned them repeatedly that you won't be that person again. Not ever. They get that." Grady sighed. How do I do this, Lord? How do I explain it so she understands? "Look at it this way. God chose us. He knows who we are. We can follow the plan He has laid it for us, or we can shift to our own. A lot of the time we go our own way. That changes who we are. He still loves us, showers us with compassion and mercies. He is faithful to us."

Eineen had turned to watch his face before she nodded. "I get that, Grady. I really do." Her head went down on his shoulder. "Can we go home, please? We can't stay with Silas and Madigan for a long time. Madigan shared with me today that they are planning their family, in fact, they will have a little one here in about six months. I don't want to endanger them anymore."

Grady was silent, his thoughts racing, before he agreed.

"I think you are right, my love. We do need to make plans." He set her on her feet, reached for her hand, and then walked towards the street. "We are going downtown to see Bill. We need to speak with him and also Sam, to plan the best way to do just that."

Her face lighting up, Eineen smiled. "You would do that?"

"As you say, we can't stay here forever. We need to go back to where you were raised, to tromp the paths and whatnot that you were familiar with. Staying here? In unfamiliar territory? Nothing here will trigger a memory that just might be the one to restore you to full health."

Grady paused as they neared the downtown, knowing that Eineen needed a rest, and pointed to a store.

"In there." He tugged her after him, her mouth dropping open as she saw what store they were in.

"Grady? You can't. You're not working right now."

Grady merely laughed, kissed her, and then asked to see the gold crosses. He wanted one for his bride. She needed it.

Chapter 17

Two days later, Grady dropped the duffle bags that Bill had handed him, to scoop Eineen into his arms, laughter on his face at her protest. Bill merely shook his head, a grin on his own face, as he took Grady's keys and unlocked the door, watching as Grady carried Eineen over the doorstep before setting her down and kissing her thoroughly. Eineen's face was rosy as she hid it against him for a moment, listening to the conversation between the two men before Bill said his goodbyes and ran for his car, dodging the now falling rain.

Grady simply stood, his heart thankful, praise raised to his Lord, that He had provided just the lady that Grady needed, and would He bless their life together? And please, dear Lord, keep my lady safe.

Eineen finally freed herself from Grady's arms and wandered through the bungalow, liking what she saw.

"Who decorated it?" She found him in the kitchen, staring at the coffee pot as it dripped. "That won't make it drip any faster, you know."

"I know. It's a habit, I guess. I pray when I stand here, for whoever comes to my mind. It's not a long time, but I can remember a few people." He turned, handing her the glass of milk he had poured.

He assumed Sam had stocked him up on groceries.

"Thank you." Eineen stood, staring at the coffee pot herself. "I like that idea. Only I don't drink coffee."

"No, but there are other things you do, that are what we consider mindless, that you can use the time to pray for someone."

Grady finally walked through his home himself, searching for anything that was off, pausing in his office before he sank down into his chair. He buried his head in his hands for a moment before he looked up and then reached for the mail. He knew his sister had taken care of bills for him, that was a given. It was a given, it's what they did for one another.

Grady sighed. That is another problem, isn't it, Lord? I have to talk to my family, introduce them to my bride, and try and explain just what has happened over the last few weeks. He knew that they would back him, but it was still unsettling for him to even think about.

His hand paused on a long envelope, his name and address handwritten, but minus a stamp. He had a horrible feeling all of a sudden, that this would just complicate things. He looked up as he heard Eineen singing quietly to herself as she unpacked for them, and then he heard the water running in the shower. He smiled. She had made herself to home, and he was glad.

Grady's finger opened the flap and he pulled out the single folded piece of paper, hesitation in his manner before he unfolded it.

"If ur readin' this, we know where u is. We will find you. U ain't gonna escape."

Grady's heart sank. It had to be Duffy or his family. Bill had said that Duffy was still in jail, that his bail was set too high for him to make, and that eased his burden somewhat, but made it worse in the same instance. He set the letter aside, knowing he would need to talk to Eineen, but also knowing he would have to call Sam, and that he didn't plan on doing that very evening. Tomorrow would work.

He reached for his phone, turning it over and over, knowing his voice mailbox was likely full. He listened to them, most of them from his family, the growing worried tone of the messages concerning him. He sent out a group text, letting them know he had been away, had not had his phone, but that he would need to talk to them. Could they do a conference call or video call? His parents were still away, he thought. The insistent chiming of his phone brought his eyes to his text message app, and he smiled, thankful he had an understanding family.

Grady paused, his eyes on the door, knowing that they had to let Eineen's parents and brother know they were around and back in town, but he didn't wish to go behind her back to do that. He rose, his phone in his hand, to search for her, finding her standing in the hallway, her gaze on a photo.

"Grady, where is that?"

"That? It's a stream on your Dad's property. I think, from what I can remember, it's near where your home is." Grady sighed. "We need to talk, my love. We need to figure out where to live."

"I know. I would suggest in town, using my place for weekends and holidays and when we want to escape." She turned, a frown on her face, seeing his phone in his hand. "You found your phone!"

"I did. Sam said he had and that he had given it to Lois to bring here. She's my youngest sister."

"Of course, you have told me that. I just forget sometimes." She walked into his open arms, relishing how cherished he made her feel. "I guess we need to approach the family that is apparently mine."

"We will. That's what I wanted to talk to you about. How be I send off a text message to Eames and get his feeling of what and when?"

Eineen shrugged, not really interested, she thought. "I guess. It won't do any harm." She moved away from him. "Do you have any food in the house?"

Grady began to laugh, catching the smirk on her face as she turned into the kitchen. "We do, my love. Sam stocked up for us. He didn't want anyone else to come through until he had searched high and low, as Bill put it."

"Searched?" Eineen's head appeared as she stepped back to look down the hall at him.

"Searched as in looking for bugs, devices, bombs, traps."

Eineen paled. "I guess he would need to do that, wouldn't he? I gather he didn't find anything." Her voice trailed away before she was suddenly backing out of the kitchen. "Grady?"

He was beside her in an instance. "What is it, Eineen?"

Raising a shaking finger, she pointed at the window over the sink. "There. Something is there. They know, Grady. They know we're back."

Grady turned her and hands on her shoulders, walked her back to his office, seating her at his desk, and then reaching for his phone.

"Sam? Hi, it's Grady. When?

About an hour ago. Listen. Eineen saw something out of the kitchen window. Are you free or are you on duty? You're free and heading this way. How did you know?" Grady gave a brief laugh. "Bill did, did he? Okay, we'll see you in a bit then. Where are we? In my office. I have a lock on the door which I will use if I have to, and I have a secret in the room that no one knows about, not even my family. No, I'm not telling."

Grady dropped his phone on the desk and then crouched down beside Eineen, an arm around her.

"Sam's on his way. He was heading this way, anyway. He'll look into what it was."

"I saw someone standing there, staring in. He had a paper in his hand that he was holding up. What did we do, Grady?" Eineen was shaking with fear

"We did what we had prayed about and what we had peace about. Coming home. It is a risk no matter

———

91

where we are. We both agree on that." He looked up and around her. "I am going to show you something that I pray you may never have to use." He stood, reaching for her hand, and helping her to stand.

Leading her to the far wall, he paused, before he reached to pull forward an ornament on the shelving. Eineen watched in surprise as the shelf moved inward and a light came on. She stepped forward, leaning to look inside.

"A hidden room?"

"It is. I want you to remember how to open it. Your life may depend on it. I have kept it stocked with water and dried foodstuffs, and there are flashlights and battery-operated lamps. I pray you never have to use it but it's here if you need to."

Grady shut the room up as he heard a tap at the front door.

"Stay here, until I call you. Be ready to dodge in there. Can you remember how to work it?"

EIneen nodded. "I can. Go. See who that is."

Chapter 18

Standing on Grady's back porch, Sam stared down at the paper that he held in his hand. How did they know? They must have been watching Gradys' place, he decided. That had to be the only way.

He turned as he heard the sound of padding feet crossing the hardwood floor and then the door opened. He smiled to himself. Grady would go barefoot as much as he could, he knew. He remembered seeing him around town as a youngster, barefoot if possible.

"Sam?" Grady's voice was quiet. "What did you find? I need to reassure Eineen, and I'm not sure that I can."

"This won't do it, that much I know." Sam stared down at the paper, ensconced as it was in an evidence bag. "They know you're here, Grady. They know Eineen is here. They know you two are married. They are threatening you because of that."

"That's what we thought would happen. How do we do this, Sam? How do I keep Eineen safe? We have to go back to as normal a life as we can. That means being out in the community, at church." Grady sighed. "And it means seeing our families. I have yet to talk to mine, to tell them what has happened. And Eineen? She needs to see hers, to reconnect with them. And I'm not sure how well that will go."

"We're bathing it in prayer, Grady. That's a given." Sam squinted at the darkening night. "Let's

———

93

get you inside. You two will need to watch the time of day you're out here. And don't tell me this is your favourite time of day and you sit out here with your coffee." He waited before he glanced over at Grady, seeing the grin on his face. "You're not saying anything."

"No. You told me not to tell you what my favourite time of day is." He laughed as he headed back inside, an arm going out to hug Eineen, before he seated her, her usual glass of milk in front of her, coffee in mugs for himself and Sam.

Sam stood just inside the closed door, having pulled the blind down on it to shut out the night and to keep the light inside. He stared at Eineen, wonder in his heart that she was back home, but fear as well, knowing they had not found all the men responsible. He had talked to Bill earlier that afternoon. Bill had told him that Duffy still had not made bail, it was still set too high for him, and whoever it was he was working for, had refused contact from him. That person they were still trying to determine the name for.

"Eineen? It is good to see you, girl. I've been worried." Sam sat, his mug of coffee in front of him, the evidence bag beside him, turned upside down. He watched as she shifted uneasily, only stilling when Grady's arm went around her.

"Hi. I understand we know each other. I'm sorry. I just don't remember." Eineen frowned at him. "But you do look familiar."

Sam grinned. "I've known you all your life, Eineen. Your Dad and I were childhood friends, growing up just a few houses apart." He took a sip of coffee, trying to regain control of his emotions. "Your Mom and Dad are anxious to see you. So is your brother."

Eineen shrugged. "I wish I could say the same, but I can't. I don't remember them. I'm sorry."

"They understand that, Eineen, and will take that into account. Now that you're back in town, we need to set something up."

Grady had been watching her face. "Can we do it somewhere neutral, Sam? Somewhere she won't feel threatened or overwhelmed?"

"That we can do. Not my place, much as we would like to. Not your parents' or Eames'. I would suggest we avoid her home in the woods. That is not safe for you, not yet. If you want to go there, let me know. I'll go with you and have some of our friends from the force accompany us as well."

"That would work, more than likely." Grady watched Eineen closely, seeing that she was relaxing with Sam, her hands stilling from clenching on her lap. He looked up at Sam, catching his nod. "Eineen, Sam found the paper that the man was holding. It was a threat. They know we're back and that we're married."

Eineen nodded, a sober look on her face. "Why is this happening? Why had God allowed it?"

"That I can't answer, my love. Nor can Sam. I am not sure anyone would be able to at this point, and it may be that we never will be able to."

Eineen nodded. "I get that. I just was asking. You know, thinking out loud. I shouldn't have. I'm sorry."

Grady's arm tightened around her. "Never apologize for asking something like this. Right now, you need to voice your thoughts, your questions, your fears. You don't know what question or reply will help. But I think Sam is right. We need to take precautions, my love. I don't want to lose you and I will if Duffy or his men get their hands on you."

Eineen had turned her head to watch him. "I know. I don't want that to happen." Her voice was a mere whisper. "But how do we go on with life?"

"We just do. We start going to places. Shopping. Church. Friends'. Our families'."

She nodded. "That's easy for you. You remember them. I don't. And right now, I don't know that I want to. What if me not remembering is the only thing keeping one of them alive?"

Chapter 19

Sam had finally left, with not much more information than he had started with. It was frustrating, Lord. How do we keep this young lady safe? And Grady too? They had finally agreed on a place, and Grady had spoken with his employer, who gladly offered his home to the families. When would they like to come, he asked. Was tomorrow too soon?

Grady had laughed and said to let him arrange something. He would be back in touch with Jim as soon as he could.

Later, Eineen stood at the kitchen sink, staring down at the water as it circled into a whirlpool shape to drain out. She felt that her life was like that, that she was caught in a whirlpool and just didn't know how to get away.

Grady's arms came around her and he pulled her back against him, his chin on her hair.

"You're lost in thought, my love."

"I am. Just thinking my life is like being in a whirlpool right now, with no way out." Eineen blinked rapidly. "How do we do this, Grady, without one of us or one of our families getting hurt? I mean, I don't remember mine, but I guess they're close to me and I must have loved them. I just don't remember that. And that must hurt them."

"It would hurt them more if you didn't survive this. And that is a possibility." Grady's heart broke for his bride. "We'll pray about it."

Eineen moved away from him, wiping off the table, setting things back to where she thought they came from, and then stood and frowned, not sure if they were in the right place. She glared at Grady as he laughed.

"Love, I don't care where you put things. All I care about is you and that you are here with me. Now, shall we spend some time in prayer? I have a Psalm I would like to share with you."

"Thank you, Grady. I need this."

Three days later, Eineen stood on Jim's front walk, frozen in place, her hand tight in Grady's, as she stared at the front door of the house. She could hear the birds and insects with their late summer songs and could smell the scent of the fresh-cut grass from somewhere in the neighbourhood.

"Are you okay, my love?" Grady's voice was low, his eyes shifting between her and Jim who stood in the open door.

"I think so. I just don't know if I can do this, Grady.

I really don't." Panic laced her words.

"If you can't, then we turn around and walk away. I will not force you to do this. It will be a decision we make together. If you feel you can't, then our decision will be made. Jim will explain to your folks."

"But what about your family? Aren't they here?"

"No, not today. We'll meet them later. Today, this is for you. For your family." Grady looked up as he heard a sound and saw Esther standing behind Jim. He shook his head at Jim, who turned, ushering Esther back into the house. "So, my love, what will we do?"

"Go forward, I guess. This is so hard. I should know them, but I don't. That scares me."

"I know it does." Grady whispered a prayer for her as he watched Jim walk towards him. "Jim. I'm glad to see you."

"Grady! I was worried. It wasn't like you to have just not reported in. I was glad to hear from Sam that you were still around." His hand came out to shake Grady's before he turned to Eineen.

"Eineen! What a relief! I know you don't remember me. That's okay. We'll get there."

Eineen gave a shy smile, not quite sure of herself. "They're in there?"

"They are. Take your time. We're in no rush." Jim paused, his mouth drawn back from his teeth for a moment. "If you can't do this today, Eineen, your father says they understand. It will be difficult for them but they do want you to be safe."

"Thank you." Eineen leaned against Grady for a moment. "It's just them?"

"That's right. Garrett, Esther, and Eames. Come in when you're ready. Grady, we're out back for now.

—

We thought it best to be in the open." Jim stared at the car parked across the street, the one that had been there for days.

"I think that you two should come in. I don't like that car over there."

Grady shifted to look over his shoulder. "I've seen it before. In the town where we were. They've tracked us down, Jim. Now that they have, I'm not sure this is such a good idea."

"Head for the house. I'll put a call into the police. Sam made me promise that I would."

Jim turned, heading for his house, not seeing the window of the car lowering or the weapon that had appeared. Grady's arm was around Eineen, leading her forward, when a sound had his head turning rapidly to look behind him. A cry was torn from him as he wrapped his arms around Eineen and dove for the ground, to lay still, his body covering hers in a protective manner.

Chapter 20

At the popping sound behind him, Jim whirled, his eyes first on the car that was rapidly speeding away, before he dropped to the ground. He heard Garrett and Eames behind him, their footsteps hurried as they ran for the front of the house.

"Stay in the house! And get down! Garrett, call 911!" Jim inched his way to the front of the porch, his eyes searching for another assailant, even as he caught a glimpse of Grady and Eineen in a huddled heap on the ground. He raised himself, stepped off the porch, and then dropped back down as a bullet sent a splinter of wood flying from near his head.

"Jim? Eineen? Grady? Are they okay?" Garrett had crawled himself out onto the deck, motioning Eames and Esther to stay inside and stay down.

"I can't tell. Whoever it is that is out there is not letting me move towards them." Jim cautiously raised his head enough to look towards the young couple. "They're are either hurt or else playing possum."

The two men could hear the rising and lowering sounds of ongoing sirens and then saw the red and blue emergency lights flickering through the neighbourhood before the cruisers squealed to a halt and the officers were out, weapons drawn, approaching the house.

"There's another shooter!" Jim raised a bit more. "To the north. From up in the tree, I think."

Some of the officers split away, some stopped by the young couple, and the others headed toward Jim and Garrett, motioning them to their feet and into the house, the door closed, an officer inside with them, another standing at the door

Sam threw his cruiser door open and ran for the yard, his heart in his mouth. This is what he had feared, that someone would attack Grady and Eineen. He rested a hand on the back of a fellow officer who was kneeling beside the couple.

"How are they?"

"He's hurt." The officer tilted his head. "Grady?"

"Yeah, Grady. He was here to meet with Eineen's parents. I was afraid of this."

"Of what? And who is he protecting?"

"Eineen. You know her."

"I do. I thought she was missing." The young officer looked up at Sam before he stood, moving back to let the paramedics take over.

"She was. Grady was with her. Just so you know, they're married." Sam scanned the area even as he continued to speak.

"Eineen? I didn't think she would marry. She was never interested in dating anyone." The young officer studied Sam's face before looking back at Eineen.

"I know. But they are married. I want patrol officers with them at all times. There have been death threats against them." Sam hesitated for a moment. "I want you with Grady. Find one of the lady officers for Eineen. Keep what I am about to tell you quiet. Eineen does not remember anything about her life before she disappeared."

The officer, Tim by name, stared at Sam. "She what?" At Sam's stern look, Tim swallowed hard. "Okay. Let me find Beth. She knows Eineen."

"Just let her know that Eineen will not recognize her.

I don't want the word spread around too much about this."

Sam watched as the ambulances finally pulled away, the senior paramedic shaking their head as he approached.

"Grady?"

"Not sure, Sam. He took at least two. Eineen? She wasn't hit by the bullets, Grady made sure of that. It's just that we can't get her to wake up."

"Keep it low key but let the treating physicians know that she was injured a few weeks ago, in a tumble down a slope. She doesn't remember anything before that. So if she acts strange with them, doesn't respond to someone she knows, that's why."

"I will. You're heading in as well?"

"Once I can clear from here. If you need me, call. I'll head in. I just need to talk to Garrett and

Esther, and then Jim. Grady's people are back, I think he said. By the way, they're married, but I don't think he's had a chance to talk to his folks."

The paramedic stared at Sam before he nodded and then ran for the paramedic rig, heading off after the ambulances. Sam sighed as he turned, to find Eineen's people and Jim standing on the porch, waiting for him.

"Sam?" Garrett's voice was laced with worry.

"She wasn't hit, Garrett. But we'll get her checked over. Grady was, in trying to protect her. How bad, I don't know yet."

"Can we leave here or do we have to remain?" Eames shifted from foot to foot, he was that anxious to see his sister.

"Soon, Eames. I will have someone take you." Sam turned to study the yard and then the surrounding homes. "I'm sorry, Jim. I thought we were safe."

"We should have been, but I think someone has been around here in the last few days. I just felt like I was being watched." Jim was frustrated, showing it by running his hands through his hair.

"Since we planned this?" At his nod, Sam sighed. "Then, someone has a listening device at Grady's. It was not planned until that night. Or else they've been watching to see if he shows up. Eineen's family being here was a dead giveaway.'

Sliding her hands along the wall behind her, Eineen backed away from the nurse standing in front of her, fear filling her in a way that she didn't think she had ever felt it. She needed Grady but he wasn't there. And no one would tell her where he was. The last thing she remembered was walking towards Jim's house, or at least, that's who she thought it was.

"Where's Grady?" Eineen's voice held the panic she was feeling.

"You can't see him right now, Eineen. Now, back up on the stretcher. The doctor wants to check you over. You can't leave just yet." The nurse reached for Eineen's arm, surprised when Eineen flung it up into the air and then darted past her, the door flying open hard enough to hit the wall before it swiftly shut again. She sighed, heading for the door, knowing Eineen would be searching for Grady, just why, the nurse could not understand.

Eineen moved at a rapid pace, searching for Grady, the panic becoming worse until she literally ran into Sam, who just gathered her into a hug like he would his own daughter.

"Sam, where's Grady? I need to see Grady."

"I know you do, Eineen. You can't. He's in imaging right now, having pictures taken. Come on. Let's you and I sit out in the waiting room." He turned her, an arm tight around her to prevent her from escaping again. "I'll stay with you. I promise. They'll come to get you as soon as they can. They know you're important to him."

Sam's calm voice helped to quiet Eineen to some extent. He directed her to a seat from which she could watch the doors, but from where she would be protected. Several officers milled around, sent there to provide protection. He nodded to Garrett, knowing Garrett and Esther wanted to be with their daughter, but held back, not knowing if they would be welcomed by her. He sat, his eyes in constant movement, before he saw Grady's parents and sister entering, heading for the clerk, before they turned back to sit, their anxiety palpable.

"Sam? Is Grady alive?" Eineen's voice was low enough that he had to bend close to hear her.

"He is, Eineen. God kept him alive. How badly he's injured? We'll know more." Sam looked up and then stood, his hand out to shake Grady's father's hand. "Isaiah. Good to see you, though I would rather it be under different circumstances."

"That is true. How is he? Your officer merely said he was hurt, and would we come."

"He was hurt, yes. Isaiah, he was shot, protecting Eineen here." Sam moved slightly to one side and Isaiah saw Eineen, a frown on his face as he watched her.

"Eineen? I don't understand, Sam. They aren't friends, not that he's ever said."

Sam sighed. "I guess it falls to me to tell you. Grady said that he was working up setting up a group call or something tomorrow."

"That's right. How did you know?" Isaiah's arm came around Lydia, his wife, as she approached, Lois, their youngest daughter, beside her.

"Grady said he hadn't talked to you. Then, you wouldn't be aware that he and Eineen were abducted, she was injured, and can't remember her family. Long story short, they're married, Isaiah. The telling of that is for those two." Sam spun as he caught a glimpse of Eineen on her feet, heading for the physician who had come out, obviously looked for her. "Excuse me." He was after her, seeing her parents on their feet, wanting to go with her, but not daring to.

"Dad? Did I hear right?" Lois stared after Eineen, not sure she had heard correctly what Sam had just said.

"If you heard what I heard, then yes. That must be what he wanted to talk to us about." Isaiah reached an arm around each of the women and led them back to a seat, his eyes not seeing Eineen's parents sitting across from them, compassion on their faces.

Sam reached to slow Eineen's pace. "Slow down, young lady. We'll get you to Grady. Just let us talk to the physician here and then we'll get you in."

The physician shared a look with Sam before he turned to Eineen. "Eineen? I understand you and Grady are married? Is that correct?" At her nod, he sighed. This is not what he had thought would be the case. In fact, he had denied it, until he saw the wedding ring on Grady's finger and now seeing the matching one of Eineen's. "Just a few minutes to chat with you. Grady's lucky. He was hit twice. One bullet winged him as we say, on the left upper arm. That's a concern but it will heal without any problems. He took another one in the lower back, but it didn't hit anything vital. It was off to one side, through muscle and fatty tissue, more to the flank area. It will take some time to heal. We've been able to patch him up without taking him to surgery. Any questions?" He watched her face, seeing the relief she had to feel, but also the fear, and that he just didn't understand.

"Can I see him? I need to. Please?" Eineen was begging and knew it, but she didn't care. All she wanted was to see Grady, to make sure he was okay, and to have him tell her she would be just fine.

"Sure. We'll take you to him. We'll be moving him upstairs soon for overnight. I understand you won't stay to be examined."

"No, I'm not important. I wasn't hurt. Grady protected me. Where is he? He's not dead, is he? That's what you're not telling me. He's dead." Eineen's face had whitened and she had begun to shake. Sam's arm went around her.

"He's not dead, Eineen. Come, let's get you to him." Sam looked over his shoulder. "His parents and sister are here."

"Are they? Then, we'll get them in as well." The physician opened his mouth to ask a question before he snapped it closed. It really wasn't any of his business, how these two were married, and how it seemed that no one knew.

Sam pushed the door open to the exam room, nodding at the officer on duty, before he ushered Eineen in with a hand to her back. He stopped, watching as she paused, hands to her mouth, before she moved forward on almost silent feet, to stand a few feet away from the stretcher, her eyes on Grady, not moving forward, frozen in place.

Grady moved restlessly, his pain rousing him, the pain medication not taking effect yet. His eyes fluttered open and he gazed around, a frown on his face. A hospital room? What had happened? Then, his thoughts flew to Eineen, and he shoved at the blankets, moving to sit before the pain had him flat on his back. He felt a hand on his and shifted, his blurry eyes finding Eineen standing behind him, shock and horror and worry on her face, her hands gripping his as tight as she could manage.

"Eineen? You're okay?" His voice was hoarse from pain, barely above a whisper.

"I am. You saved me." Anger flared momentarily. "Don't do it again. I could have lost you."

His free hand reached to touch her face. "I would do it again in a heartbeat, my love. You're sure you're okay?"

"I am. You were shot, you know." Eineen sounded disgruntled about that fact.

A small smile creased Grady's face, even as his vision began to fade, the medications kicking in at last. "I gathered that. Don't leave me, Eineen. Stay with me."

Chapter 22

Holding the door to Grady's room open, Isaiah hesitated to enter. Lydia and Lois had been in and then headed home, leaving Isaiah to find Eineen and talk with her. That was not something he was looking forward to. How did you talk to a young lady who had become your daughter-in-law without you being aware of it? *Grady, what did you do, son? I know your heart. I am sure you are in love with her, but so quickly. Lord, help me to understand. Help me to show mercy and compassion to this young lady who I understand doesn't remember anything about her town or her people.*

Eineen looked up from where she had seated herself near the window, fear wafting through her, before she frowned. She knew this man. For some reason, she could remember him.

"Mr. Michaels?" Her voice was soft, soft enough not to awaken Grady, but also soft enough that Isaiah had trouble hearing her until he walked forward.

A frown on his face, he glanced at her before looking at Grady, his steps stopping by his son's bed. He watched the restless movements, thankful that Grady was still with them. It could have been so much worse.

"Mr. Michaels?" Eineen had arisen, to come to stand beside Isaiah, a hand on his arm.

"Eineen? You're all right, lass?" At her nod, he frowned. "But you called me by name. I didn't think you remembered."

Eineen sighed. "I don't remember a lot but I remember you. You're Grady's father, and his best friend, he tells me. He is a wonderful, compassionate, caring man. You have set that example for him. I know from what I have seen and heard about you."

Isaiah was puzzled, to put it mildly. "I gather Grady doesn't know you remember me."

Eineen's eyes were on Grady, who had awakened at the sound of his father's voice but kept still, listening to the conversation. A smile lit her face. "He didn't but he does know. Grady? How are you? Do you need more meds?"

Grady shook his head, his eyes on his father. "Dad?" His voice was hesitant.

"It's okay. Sam spoke with us. I gather this is what we were meeting about tomorrow? To tell your Mom and me that we had added another lovely young daughter to our family?" He grinned, the youthful look on his face reminding Eineen of Grady when he was teasing her.

"It was. I wish it was different, Dad. God led there, I think."

"You think?" Eineen's voice held pretended outrage. "You'd better be positive on that, buster."

Grady grinned. "I am, my love. That I am." He looked past them towards the door. "Mom?"

"She and Lois were in a while ago. She's headed home to call Dorcas. I am sure Dorcas will be here tomorrow."

Grady groaned. "I am sure she will be. Eineen, my love, do I get to go home tomorrow?"

"You do. As long as you behave tonight." She smirked at his grin, Isaiah watching closely, before his heart raised in thankfulness.

She's just who he needs, isn't he, Lord? You planned this. Thank you. He finally turned and walked away, leaving the young couple to stare after him before looking at each other and shrugging.

"Sam has been around, Grady. He wanted to talk to you, but he was going off duty. He's away tomorrow." Eineen paced, her arms wrapped around herself, before she turned, finding Grady had levered himself upright and was holding out an arm for her, knowing she needed the contact with him that would be the only thing to calm her. She flew to him, carefully cradling close, their arms around one another.

"I thought I had lost you. I thought you were dead when they wouldn't let me see you." Her tears finally fell, tears she had not wept in all the time she had been in danger.

"Ssh, my love. It's okay. Weep. I understand. God gives us tears for healing." He began to pray, feeling her relaxing as he did so.

"Are you sure you're okay?"

"I am. The doctor said I need to take it easy for a couple of weeks. Jim was in. He has work in the office I can do, or I can work from home. I can access the programs I need, and anything I need from the office, he'll make sure I get."

"But you are supposed to be out investigating or tracking or something, aren't you?" Eineen was not clear in what it was exactly that Grady did. She felt his body shaking with suppressed laughter. "Behave or I'll tell the nurse on you."

Grady kissed her to silence her before he leaned back on the bed that she had raised. "You do my heart so much good, my love."

"About your family. I remembered your Dad without him saying anything. Why?"

Grady stared at her before he shrugged. "You did? I don't know why. I guess it can happen like that. Dad was pleased with God's choice for me."

"He was?" Her brow wrinkled as she puzzled through his words. "How do you know that?"

"By how he welcomed you. He would not have called you another lovely young daughter if he had had any reservations. Did you see my mom and Lois?"

"No, that was when I was out with Sam. Giving the statement to an officer that he seemed to think I needed to." Eineen was exhausted, the physical strain of the day weighing heavy on her, the emotional strain even more so. Her eyes closed as her head turned on Grady's shoulder and she slept.

The nurse appeared, chart in hand, stopping for a moment before she looked up at Grady.

"She's asleep. I need to wake her. She can't stay there."

"No, you leave her. I'll answer for it. You don't understand. She needs to be with me."

The nurse finally shrugged, and as she left, kept looking back over her shoulder. She would certainly be making a call to the physician in charge of Grady's care. This was not to be. She was shocked when she was told to leave Eineen be, that the authorities had cleared it with him, and it was really documented in his chart if she would only read it. She did, and sat back, anger briefly rising in her. She would make that couple pay for her being told off as she had been. Her eyes were raised to the officer on guard and then sighed. Somehow, she didn't think that it would be tonight, but she would not forget. At some point, she would exact that revenge.

Chapter 23

Staring at his mother the next day, Grady kept an arm around Eineen, feeling her tense as she faced Lydia, not sure about what to expect. Grady's heart broke for his lady, knowing she wanted to remember his family and hers, but something just kept blocking it.

"Mom, please. This is Eineen's home and mine. She has the say of what happens. I'm sorry. I know you mean well." Grady hated to speak to his mother in such a manner but he had to set the tone.

"I'm sorry, Grady. It's just so new. Eineen, forgive me, please? It's been a shock, to say the least. Hearing that Grady was injured and then finding out you were married, it will take a bit."

Eineen stared at her mother-in-law, a vague recollection of kindness shown to her as a child tickling at the edge of her memories. She moved away from Grady towards Lydia, Grady standing watching her, an arm wrapped around his abdomen.

"It's okay. Really. I'm not sure that I would be so gracious if I were in your shoes." Eineen reached to hug Lydia, surprising both of them. "Thank you for raising such a wonderful, caring, compassionate, Godly man." Her voice was low enough that only Lydia heard her.

With those words, Eineen had endeared herself to Lydia, without realizing she had done so.

Sam approached, his hand going under Grady's arm, steadying the younger man.

"Let's get you off your feet, Grady. I need to talk with both of you. There will be a detective around later, and I hear tell Bill or Andrew are heading this way."

"They are? Why?" Grady sank gratefully down onto the couch, his hand reaching to pull Eineen down with him.

"I have no idea. All Bill said was that they needed to talk to you and talk to you today."

"Duffy's out?"

Sam shrugged. "Not that I am aware of."

Grady tucked Eineen under his arm as she slipped to a seating position beside him, her eyes on Sam.

"No, not Duffy. One of his sons. He has, what, four?" Eineen's voice held conviction that she was right.

Sam stared at her. "You remember that?"

"I do. If I recall, they would be older than Grady and myself." She turned her head to find Grady watching her. "I think I can remember seeing them around town. Just shards of memories, mind you. And I can remember all the younger women disappearing into stores or cars or homes when they would come around." She turned back to Sam, distress on her face.

"There were a couple of girls, in their late teens, the same age as me. I can remember, now that I am starting to, that they disappeared just as they turned eighteen. I don't remember ever seeing them again."

"Let me have their names, Eineen. We'll look into it. You think it was Duffy's sons?"

"I do. Oh, please, Lord, just let them have left town."

Grady stared down at her bowed head before he looked up at Sam. "If I remember, there were some younger women around Eineen's age in their camp. You don't suppose, do you?"

"That's a possibility that we will look into. I am so sorry, Grady, Eineen. Perhaps if we had known earlier, you two wouldn't have been put in danger."

"I don't know as that would have been the case. Eineen indicated that one of our first captors used to work for her father and that he had had to fire him. Jim seems to think that Duffy's group is the one behind the illegal hunting, but I think it goes well beyond just that."

"It does. I'm not at liberty to say, but it does. I pray that you two stay out of his clutches." Sam looked up as Lydia handed him a mug of coffee from the tray she held before she sat beside Eineen, a hand reaching for one of Eineen's.

"Eineen? Have you talked to your parents?" Her question was soft.

"No, I don't remember them or Eames, is it?" She looked up. "That's what we were to do yesterday, and look how that turned out. How did they know, Sam? Who told on us?"

Sam shook his head. "That we're not sure of. I am having a tech come through your house today, with your permission. There may be a listening device or two that we don't know about."

"Or else, knowing Jim, they just took a guess that we might show up, or else they were watching Eineen's parents and followed them." Grady was frustrated.

"It was too well planned, Grady, for it to be just a chance they saw and took. There was a sniper in the tree beside Jim's house. Jim and Garrett were kept pinned down from getting to you two until the officers arrived."

Grady paled at the thought. "A sniper? That doesn't sound like Duffy. Too sophisticated."

"That's our thought. We have suspicions that Duffy is not working on his own, that he is working for someone else."

"That would be the case. That has been the rumour all along, hasn't it?" Eineen's eyes slid closed, shudders shaking her body, as the memories started to flood back to her mind. She didn't hear Grady's voice calling her, the agony in it not lost on his companions.

Lydia was on her feet, heading for her phone, intent on calling for Eineen's mother, when Sam stopped her.

"Lydia? Don't call Esther. That has to be Grady's call." He watched with compassion as she stopped, her eyes sliding closed.

"I'm doing it again, aren't I? After I said I wouldn't." She turned as she heard the doorbell, heading that way, Sam right behind her.

Pulling open the door, Lydia stood, shock on her face at seeing Esther and Garrett standing there, Eames right behind them.

"Esther? How did you know?" Lydia beckoned them in, Sam frowning at her as she did so.

"Know what?" Esther exchanged a puzzled look with Garrett.

"That you're needed here." Lydia shot a glance behind her, Sam frowning at Eineen's parents and brother.

"We are? Something compelled us to come. It had to be God." Esther looked around Lydia. "Where is she?"

Lydia stepped back. "In the living room. That way."

Esther dropped her purse and jacket on the dark wood table in the hallway and then headed for the living room, from where she could hear voices. She hesitated about approaching her daughter, until Grady looked up, relief on his face as he briefly raised a hand to beckon her forward. She dropped to the couch beside her daughter, eyes glued to Eineen's face, just waiting, before she reached for a hand, finding Eineen's hand gripping hers in return.

Eineen turned, sensing someone new beside her, her eyes widening for a moment before she struggled to free herself from Grady's arms, reaching for her mother.

"Mom!" Her tears began to flow in earnest as she was gathered into her mother's arms, not seeing the tears on Esther's face as she hugged her daughter tightly, or the tears of the faces of the others as they watched. Grady's hand rested on her back, as he desperately prayed for healing for her and for peace.

Chapter 24

A couple of hours later, Grady stood on the back porch, arm wrapped around his abdomen to try and ease the pain from the wound, his eyes focused on his yard. Something was off, he thought. There is something different there, but I can't place it. He turned slightly as he heard the black door close and his father and Eames approached him. Garrett had left with Sam, on a mission to investigate something in his office, just what, they had not said.

"Grady? How are you, son?" Isaiah's hand rested briefly on Grady's shoulder. He was aware that his son was struggling spiritually right then, questioning why things had happened as they had.

"To tell you the truth, Dad? I am really not sure." Grady sighed, fatigue washing over him. "I'm hurting in ways I didn't think I ever could. Does that make sense?" He looked up to see Eames nodding.

"It does, son. You've been through a lot in the last few weeks. Your emotions are all over the place, I would suspect. Facing what you two have faced? That has been a challenge that none of us really know what it's like. To have your bride not knowing who she was? That too has been difficult. I see you struggling, but I also see you trusting God more and more. Is that correct?"

Grady shrugged. "I guess. I haven't really had time to think about it, not a whole lot." He looked over at Eames, finding him staring down the yard, a closed expression on his face. "Eames?"

Eames looked over at him and then shrugged. "I'm sorry, Grady. I just don't get it. I'm not sure I ever will. Why?"

"Why? That's what Sam is working on." Grady turned as he heard the door opening again and then was stretching out his hand to shake both Bill's and Andrew's hands. "Both of you? This can't be good. Where's Silas?"

Andrew grinned. "He had a wedding or he would certainly have been here. Our ladies insisted they had to come. And no, Bill did not bring his son. Madigan has him for them."

"I see. Dad, these two men are friends. And police officers. Actually, Andrew McBeth here is chief in the town of Elmton and Bill Buckley is a detective, chief detective now, isn't it?"

Bill grinned in turn. "Someone squealed, did they? Yes. It's good to meet you two. Where can we talk, Grady?"

"My office. Do you need Eineen to join us?"

Andrew and Bill shared a look before Bill shook his head. "Not at present. We will need to speak to her. Right now, she looks emotionally wiped. Let her have some time with Phoebe and Cora. They can help. If they can't, we know plenty of other ladies she can talk to and their husbands are all willing to talk with you, if needed."

Eames stared at the three men before exchanging a glance with Isaiah, a puzzled look on his face. Grady saw it and took pity on him.

"These two gentlemen had what they term as an adventure, as did Silas that I mentioned. And how many other friends?"

"Too many." Andrew replied, not wanting to name how many he knew who had been through things, and had almost lost each other or had been seriously hurt.

Grady pointed down the hall as they entered the kitchen. "Find seats for yourselves. I'll grab coffee for us if you wish. Andrew, do you want tea instead?"

"That would be great." Andrew watched the other men head for Grady's office before he spoke. "What happened? Eineen looks rough, and you're not moving too well."

Grady stepped to the doorway, listening for a moment, hearing the quiet conversation from the living room, his lady's voice subdued, which broke his heart. He moved back towards Andrew, digging into the cupboard to find the squares and cookies that Eineen had baked, was it only yesterday morning, he thought?

"We had set up a meeting yesterday afternoon at my employer's home, to meet with her parents. We never even got in the door! Do you understand that, Andrew? We never got past the front yard. We were ambushed. I was shot, twice, and, yes, I will heal, but what it has done to Eineen, I am having trouble dealing with. Her parents showed up this morning, just as Sam and Mom were here. Eineen had started to remember her past. Thank God her mom was here. She needed her. But, yesterday? Sam told me that Jim and her Dad couldn't get to us. A sniper was pinning them down."

Andrew's eyes lifted as he saw movement in the hall and watched as Eineen moved into the kitchen, her arms coming around Grady, even as he buried his head against her. She watched Andrew carefully, not quite sure of him anymore. She felt betrayed, but by who, she just didn't know.

"Eineen?" Andrew's voice was soft, catching her attention and bringing her eyes back to him. "What are you thinking?"

Eineen shrugged. "Frankly, Andrew, I have no idea what to think. How am I supposed to know that? For one thing, I have never faced something like this before. This whole situation has upended my world. I lost time with my family that I will never get back, as has Grady. How do we deal with someone who threatens us and that we can't see? How do we protect each other or even ourselves? How restricted will our lives become? I can't live like that." Anger sparked from her eyes.

Andrew watched her carefully before he nodded. Good, he thought, she's starting to feel emotions.

That will help her heal. God, please? They need You.

"We understand that, Eineen. I know how that is first hand, as does Phoebe. So do Bill and Cora. Silas and Madigan. Talk to us at any time, we don't care if it's the middle of the night. That goes for you too, Grady." Andrew reached for the tray with the mugs of coffee and his tea and the plate of goodies on it. "I'll be in your office, Grady. Come find us." With that, he walked away, leaving the younger couple staring after him.

"Did he just do that?" Eineen's voice was barely audible, she was in shock at Andrew's movements.

"He did, my love. And he's right. We can talk to them. They will understand when our families won't." He stared down at her beloved face. "Getting better?"

Eineen shrugged. "I really don't know, anymore, Grady. I just don't know what I'm to feel or not feel." She looked up at him. "What about you?"

He shrugged in turn, a grin tugging at the corner of his mouth, as he copied her actions. "I don't know either. All we can do, my love, is keeping praying and trusting, no matter how hard it gets. God is gracious. He is compassionate. He is merciful. And He is faithful. Keep that in mind."

"Do we know someone who could make us a poster with those words?"

"We can do it ourselves. You can design, and Jim will print it out at work for us." An arm around her, he turned her towards the living room. "Go on, my love. Go talk to the ladies. Bill and Andrew have some stuff to go over with us, but for now, they said they don't need you in on the meeting."

She huffed at him, her eyes narrowing as she caught him trying to hide his grin. She reached up,

kissed him, and then walked away, a smirk on her face
as he laughed.

Chapter 25

Late that night, Eineen settled down into the swing on the back porch, her toe shoving against the floor to set it in motion, her inevitable glass of milk in her hand. Her head went back against it as she studied the night sky, watching the clouds scudding over the stars and the moon, hearing the night sounds, sounds that helped her to relax. She didn't stir as Grady slipped down beside her, his hand reaching for her glass to set it on the table beside her, before he wrapped an arm around her, snuggling close to her.

Grady finally spoke, his voice soft in the night air, his attention searching for anything that shouldn't be there.

"You okay, my love?"

Eineen shrugged. "I'm not sure. I'm not sure how I'm supposed to feel. Not anymore." She shifted on the seat, turning so she could study him, watching his profile. "Did you know Mom was coming today?"

Grady shook his head. "None of us did. They just showed up." He turned his face towards her, reaching to kiss her before he spoke again. "I was glad she was. You needed her. That was what they call a God moment, I think, my love."

"It was." Her head went back down on his shoulder. "Grady, where do we go from here? Andrew and Bill really didn't help. Not with what they threw at us."

"No, they didn't, but that's who they are. They make sure we have the information we need, to make the decisions we need, and that they need to make for us and with us. Sam has been kept apprised of it all, I know. I didn't expect them to name who they did."

"Nor me. But you know, I have had suspicions about him all my life. I just never felt comfortable around him. And he goes to the church." Eineen groaned. "Tomorrow is Sunday. Can we skip church?"

Grady gave a low laugh. "We could. I could use the excuse that I'm injured, but we need to be there, love."

"I know." Eineen sounded disgruntled and unhappy before she sighed, a sigh drawn from deep within her. "I'm sorry. That was uncalled for. Lord, work on my attitude, please? I just want this over, and it just doesn't seem that it will ever be."

Grady's eyes had slid closed as she spoke, his heart breaking, but knowing that this was all part of the healing process for her. His head turned as his eyes popped open as a soft skiff of sound, before he froze, his arm tightening around Eineen, who had jumped at the sound.

"Don't make a move, either one of you." The voice was disguised, and both Grady and Eineen tried to identify it, recognizing in it a voice that they should know.

"What do you want?" Grady was worried, no, scared, he thought, frightened that Eineen would be taken from him and he would never find her again.

"I know who is behind this, behind your kidnapping, behind the shooting. It's not who you think. I know who that is, but it isn't him." The voice halted before it continued. "I am leaving something in your mailbox. Wait for an hour before you look for it. I can't guarantee your safety if you don't." The voice stopped and they heard the barest whisper of sound as the speaker disappeared.

Eineen spun on the seat, her mouth opening and closing before she stared at Grady.

"Did that really just happen?"

"It did." Grady's hand held her in place. "Wait. Let him have a few moments to get away. We'll go in soon. And then, I'll walk around the house, just to check. It wouldn't be unusual for me to do so."

"Grady, you need to be in bed. It's late and you just came home from the hospital!" Eineen groaned. "Was that only today?"

"It was." Grady stood, a hand out for Eineen, reaching for her glass of milk, before he walked them into the house, locking the door behind them.

Eineen stood just inside the front door, which she insisted had to stay open, as Grady walked the yard and around the house, the beam from his flashlight flickering in the dark. He paced up the stairs, stopping for a moment to reach into the mailbox, before he headed towards Eineen, sweeping the door close and then sweeping his bride into his arms, feeling her shaking in fear.

"What was in the box?" Her question was muffled against him.

Grady turned her, heading them towards his office. "In here, my love. Let's open whatever it is in here." He shoved her into his chair and then placed the package on the desk, reaching for his letter opener, pausing at the look on her face. He made a sound, reached instead to scoop Eineen into his arms, and then sat down in the chair, a grin on his face at her small squeal before she scolded him for lifting her.

Eineen poked at the envelope with a long forefinger, not wanting to know what was inside but also knowing that they had to look at it. There was no doubt in her mind that what was they would be doing. She heard Grady praying before his hand reached for the end of the envelope he had opened and then lift it to dump out the contents. They both stared at it and then at one another.

"What were we given?" Eineen was in shock, to put it mildly, staring at the papers, some legal, the photos, and the thumb drive.

"I have no idea." Grady reached around her to use both hands, sorting the information, his hands stopping as Eineen reached for his.

"Her?"

Grady frowned. "Her? Who?"

"Betty Graves. She was your nurse last night. She certainly didn't like me in the room." Eineen sat back against him, her hands finding his. "Do you know her?"

Grady shook his head. "No, I don't. Should I?"

"Maybe not, but Mom knows her. She's mentioned for years how Betty seemed to have it in for her."

Eineen paled, drawing in her breath sharply, causing Grady's attention to shift abruptly from his desk to her.

"Eineen?" His voice held worry and concern.

"She's Duffy's youngest sister. How could I have forgotten that, but then last night, I wasn't remembering too much." She paused, a frown appearing on her face that Grady just wanted to wipe away. "I remembered your Dad. How did I do that when I couldn't remember my own parents? And this morning, I remembered your Mom, well, sort of." She gave Grady a playful slap on the arm as he snickered. "Behave, buster."

"That just sounded so positive, my love. But it is strange that you would remember Dad." Grady gave a deep sigh to cover the pain he was experiencing, but he could not hide his discomfort from Eineen.

Eineen swept everything back into the envelope and then stood, her hand reaching for Grady's, to pull him to his feet."You're in pain, Grady, and don't try and hide it. It's past time for your pain medications and then you need to be off your feet and sleeping."

Grady nodded, a grimace of pain crossing his face. "You're right, my love. I'll lock that envelope in the safe and then head for bed. I've locked up everything." He walked away, his movement slow

enough to that Eineen was concerned but she knew she
could not hover over him.

Chapter 26

Monday afternoon found Eineen once more in Grady's office, the envelope she had asked him to retrieve from the safe on his desk, the contents dumped out. She sorted the material into piles, and then lifted the thumb drive, her mind on what it would hold. She didn't see Grady hovering in the doorway before he passed by, heading for the kitchen.

Grady squinted at the clock, noting it was mid-afternoon. He desperately wanted to dress up, take his bride out for a nice meal, but he knew he just wasn't up to it. He reached instead for his phone and called a friend who had a catering business. Stephen gladly agreed to cater a meal for him, and why hadn't he told him he was married? Grady just laughed, said it had happened so quickly because he didn't want to let Eineen escape. At the name, he heard silence on the other end of the phone and opened his mouth to speak when Stephen spoke.

"Eineen? Oh, terrific. She is such a wonderful lady, and you two suit each other. If I had known you were interested in her, I would have introduced you two."

Grady laughed. "I didn't know I was until we ran into danger. And to keep her safe, I felt I had to."

"You prayed about this, didn't you?" At Grady's yes, Stephen sighed. "I knew it. God was working there. I have heard rumours that she was in danger.

134

Now, that puts you in danger." He hung before Grady could even ask what he meant.

Eineen stood, hesitating in the doorway, her eyes on Grady as he stood, staring down at his phone he had laid on the kitchen counter, before she looked around the room, liking the soft creams and browns he had chosen with the odd touch of teal to add a contrast.

Grady looked up at that point, his eyes not focusing on Eineen until she spoke.

"Grady? That thumb drive? I don't want to look at it using your computer, just in case."

"I agree." He walked towards her, his hand reaching for hers, walking back to his office. "I called Sam earlier, let him know what we had. He wasn't too happy that we hadn't called him on Saturday night." He stood, staring down at his desk, feeling Eineen's arms come around him. "I'm scared, Eineen. More scared than I have ever been in my life, and I have faced some scary situations in my work." He hugged her back, his cheek resting against her head. "I am scared that something will happen to you, that I will lose you."

"God is in control, Grady. He knows the path we are walking. He is faithful to us on our walk. What happens to us? He has allowed. It may not be what we would choose, but it is in His plan for us."

Grady nodded. "You are so wise, my love. It's not easy to accept that. I fight it all the time."

"And I do, too." Eineen pointed to his desk. "What about that?"

"Sam said that he's coming to get it. But first, I really wanted to take you out to dinner." He looked down as she made a sound, a finger coming up to rest against her lips. "I know, my love. We can't. But Stephen has agreed to cater a meal for us here."

"He has? You know Stephen? Of course, you do. He knows everyone in town." She looked around for a moment, and then back up at him. "How dressy?"

Grady laughed. "As dressy as you want, as long as I can wear a suit and not my tux. I don't think I could handle that."

Eineen's face fell. "I keep forgetting. You make me do that, you know? You're supposed to be an invalid but you sure don't act like one."

Grady shouted with laughter, his hand going to brace his side. "Don't make me laugh. It hurts."

"Serves you right. What time will he be here?"

"About an hour. Hey, wait! We can't dress up!" He had forgotten that she had not retrieved her clothes from her own home.

"And why not? Eames brought in my clothes yesterday for me. He said he cleared out the closets and the dressers." She smirked at him, seeing his grin. "So, there, buster. We can so dress up." She sashayed away, leaving him laughing at her comments.

Early that evening, Grady and Eineen walked the yard, hand in hand, no conversation necessary. She had laughed when he had undone the top button of his shirt, loosened his tie, but kept his suit coat on, losing his socks and shoes. He had grinned, told her she needed to lose her heels, and feel the grass under her feet. She had stared at him and then taken him up on the dare, her low heels tossed to lie beside his shoes.

Eineen's steps grew slower and slower, as she fought nausea, a headache, and then dizziness. Her hand went to her head and she gave a low cry, before she collapsed, her hand torn from Grady's. Grady's attention had been on something odd at the end of the yard and he jerked when he felt Eineen's hand leave his, to stand for a moment, staring down at her before he was on his knees, an agonized cry torn from him, rolling her to her back, frantically feeling for a pulse.

Grady was on his feet, gathering Eineen into his arms, running for the house, tripping over their shoes, fumbling for the doorknob, before he was laying her on the couch, rushing to find one of their phones and then calling for help. He knelt beside her, a hand on her cheek, the other hand clutching hers, unable to form the words to pray but knowing that God heard the pleas of his heart.

He was on his feet, running for the door, pulling it open as he heard the sirens cut off outside the house, pointing to the living room.

"I don't know what happened. We were walking in the backyard when she collapsed." He stood, watching, shifting from foot to foot, unable to settle himself to stay still, a hand rubbing at his face, the other holding his side. He tried to damp down the panic he was feeling but was unsuccessful.

"What did she eat, Grady?" The older paramedic, Leroy, turned to him, even as he reached for the heart monitor, his partner reaching for the oxygen.

"We had a nice roast beef dinner. Stephen catered it especially for me. We both had the same." Grady paused. "No, we didn't. Not for dessert. Stephen sent a selection of treats and slices of pies and cakes. Eineen had the lemon pie. I had a piece of chocolate cake."

"Okay." Leroy watched the heart monitor, not liking what he was seeing. "What did you drink? And I know it wasn't anything alcoholic."

"No. I had my usual coffee. Eineen drinks milk, very rarely a cup of tea, or juice. She had milk tonight." Grady stared at Leroy and then towards the kitchen, with half a mind of reaching into the fridge and pulling out the container of milk and dumping it down the drain, just in case that had been the culprit.

"OK. Does she have any allergies to any foods, substances, anything?" Leroy was running a checklist in his mind, even as he and his partner worked on Eineen, a glance exchanged that told each other just how desperate a situation she was in.

"None." Grady sank to his knees, his hands rubbing at his face. "How is she?"

"She's in trouble, Grady. I can't and won't lie to you. We know each other well. Anything else that you can think of that she might have been exposed to? Chemicals? Perfumes? Anything?"

"Nothing." Grady rose as he watched them carefully transfer Eineen to the stretcher before he turned and ran for the kitchen, yanking open the fridge door, and grabbing the container of milk, before he was shoving his feet into shoes and then running after the stretcher. He shoved the milk container at Leroy. "Here. Take this. It might be the answer. I can't think of anything else she might have been exposed to or eaten. We haven't been out of the house since I came home from the hospital Saturday."

"Saturday? Why were you in there? Sit there."

Leroy pointed to the front corner of the back of the rig.

"I was shot, twice on Friday, trying to protect Eineen." Grady's eyes slid shut. "This is just getting worse and worse, you know."

Leroy shot him a look before his hands reached for the IV, to adjust the drip, and then for his stethoscope, the siren rising and falling as they headed for the hospital.

"Shot? Protecting Eineen? Grady, what did you go and do?"

"Me? Fell in love and wanted to protect my bride, that's all. She's in danger, Leroy." Grady stared at Eineen, seeing how still she was laying, and that scare him. "I need to talk to Sam Douglas."

"We can arrange that. We had to put in a call, Grady, you understand? If Eineen was poisoned, then the police have to be involved." Leroy watched Grady until he nodded before he sighed. This was not going to go well for Grady, he thought. Eineen poisoned? Grady alone with her? That had all the earmarks of

Grady being guilty or being set up. He would wager anything that it was the latter, but how did the police prove that? He was glad it was them and not himself.

———

Chapter 27

His eyes not leaving the doors to the examination rooms, Grady paced, unable to sit for more than a few seconds before he was on his feet again, pacing the waiting room, moving around the chairs and people in it. He didn't see Sam as he stood watching Grady before his eyes moved to the woman standing near the entrance, her gaze focused on Grady, a look of utter hatred on her face. He frowned. He should know her but he wasn't sure it was who he thought it was.

Sam finally walked towards Grady, stepping into his path to stop his forward walk, a hand out to steady him. Grady stared at him, not recognizing him at first.

"Sam? You're here? I thought you were away." Grady moved to pass him, but Sam's hand on his wrist kept him in place.

"Come, sit with me, Grady." Sam motioned to some chairs that were isolated from the others. "Right here. They'll see you when they come for you. I have an officer with Eineen. Now, talk to me."

Grady ran his hands through his hair for what number of times it was, he didn't know. He looked past Sam towards the doors, not seeing his father and Garrett approaching him, stopping when Sam shook his head.

"Grady? Come now. Talk to me. Tell me what happened."

"I don't know what happened. We ate a very nice catered roast beef dinner, had dessert, and then were walking in the yard. She just seemed to walk slower and slower and then she collapsed. She didn't say anything, Sam. I didn't see her in distress or discomfort, but something down the yard had taken my attention." He looked up, total devastation on his face. "Why didn't I know? Why didn't I see that she needed me?"

Sam shook his head. "I can't answer that, Grady. I don't think any of us can." He sighed. "Grady, I need to ask you some very difficult and serious questions. It's what we have to do in cases like this."

Grady's head swung around at the serious tone in Sam's voice, and he paled even more. "You think I did this? That I tried to kill her?" His voice was low as he almost hissed the words at Sam. "I wouldn't do that, Sam. I love her too much." His head dropped into his hands, his elbows resting on his thighs. "I couldn't, Sam."

"That may be, Grady, but I still have to ask the hard questions. I would rather do it here, where you can be available if you need to be, but if necessary, I'll have to take you downtown." Sam waited until Grady nodded. "Okay. Once more, tell me what you did today."

Grady sighed, his eyes on the door to where he knew his beloved bride lay, not knowing if she was alive or dead. Why, God, was his constant cry. Why did You let this happen to her?

Sam led Grady through the events of the day, up until when Eineen had collapsed. He dug deep, asking the hard questions that he knew he had to. He knew Grady hadn't done whatever it was that had caused Eineen to collapse, but he had to ask. He had to have it in writing, in Grady's statement.

"You mentioned that you had a package for me. What was in it?" Sam looked up from his notebook.

"Pictures. Notes. Receipts. And a thumb drive." Grady's voice stilled and he shot Sam a look. "The thumb drive. Eineen is the only one who touched it. I didn't. She said she had handled it, had almost stuck it into one of the USB ports but changed her mind. She didn't want to damage my computer, not when I needed it for work, and she thought there might be a virus or rogue program on it. Was there something in it?"

"We'll look at that. I have an officer going over your house right now. Your mother is there, she opened up for us. And no, she is not in the house. She can't be." Sam looked down at his copious notes. "We'll test the thumb drive. You said you grabbed the container of milk. Why?"

"Because it was the only thing that I could think of that might have been tampered with. We were bad in the last couple of days. We would be in the backyard but never locked the front door. Anyone could have come in or out."

"Not a good idea, Grady, not with what you two have been facing. What did you see down the yard that had your attention?" Sam waited, opening his mouth to ask again, when Grady turned to him.

"I'm not sure, Sam. I didn't get down that far to find out. It just seemed that something was off. Maybe something was there that shouldn't have been, or something was moved. I can't rightly say." Grady shook his head, his mind focusing on the yard. "I have felt like something was different out there since we came home. I searched but I didn't see what was triggering it. It's as if it was so subtle, I could see it but not recognize it. Does that make sense?"

"It could do. I'm having officers search the yard. How familiar is your mother with the yard?"

Grady snorted, causing Sam to stare at him in surprise.

"Mom designed it and planted it for me when I moved into the house. She has changed things around over the years, so if she's still there, she's the best one to ask."

Sam's phone was out as he called in to their dispatch, relaying his request to the dispatcher. He pocketed his phone, his eyes on Isaiah and Garrett, who had taken seats nearby but not close enough to hear what was being said.

"At some point, Grady, I will need you to come downtown." He raised a hand as Grady's head swung around. "Just as a matter of routine. I'll need you to give a formal statement. This should be done as soon as we can."

"I can't leave Eineen. Sam, I just can't." Grady was on his feet, heading for the doors as they opened and the physician appeared, his hand up to beckon Grady to go with him.

Chapter 28

His steps hesitant as he approached the stretcher, Grady studied the equipment surrounding Eineen, not hearing the explanation given to him. His hand reached for hers, the one that didn't have the IV line running to it before his other hand laid against her cheek, feeling the straps holding the ventilator mask to her face. Tears gathered in his eyes as he studied her white face, the blue lips, and then raised to study the monitors, not that he understood them, he thought. He felt a hand on his shoulder and looked to the side.

The physician stood there, compassion on his face, not quite sure how to talk to Grady or what he could tell him. Frankly, he thought, they didn't know much, other than Eineen had been poisoned and that she might not make it. Who did this, he wondered?

"Doctor? What can you tell me?" Grady's voice was broken, the tears barely contained.

"She is in rough shape, Grady. Thanks to you for thinking of the milk. We suspect that was the manner she ingested the poison. We're running some tests and the police have taken some as well to their lab. Right now? She's holding on. Until we can determine what she was poisoned with and find the antidote, I can't hold out hope for you. She may not make it, Grady. I'm sorry." His words stopped as sobs shook Grady's body. This shouldn't be happening, he thought.

Grady was finally able to nod, his attention on Eineen, his pleas for her to be healed raised to Heaven. Then, they changed. It became pleas that God's will be done. If it meant Eineen didn't make it, he would have to accept that, but he wasn't sure he could.

Grady sat, much later, in the waiting room outside the ICU, waiting for what he wasn't sure. Sam had dragged him, reluctantly, downtown to take his statement, not telling Grady that his whole house was being searched. That was a conversation they would have in the morning. Sam had returned to the hospital with Grady, finding another officer just coming on duty to follow them. He couldn't leave Grady on his own. Regardless of his feelings, Grady was still a suspect in Eineen's poisoning, until it could be proven conclusively that he was not the culprit. Sam's feelings could not get in the way of the truth coming out.

Isaiah stood for a moment, in the doorway, watching his son, knowing that Eineen's people were there, but his focus was on the hurting boy in front of him. He sat beside his son, unable to make it better for him, not this time, not like he could when Grady was a youngster and had been hurt.

Grady shifted in his chair, the pain from his wound gnawing at him. He had been ignoring it, his mind on Eineen, but he could not any longer do that. His face had whitened over the course of the evening into the early morning hours. Dark circles showed under his bloodshot eyes.

"Son? Do you have your pain medications?" Isaiah's voice reached through to Grady.

"No, I don't, Dad. And I can't get them. Mom called. We're still not allowed into the house." His agonized eyes turned to his father. "Do they really think I did this? That I would harm Eineen?"

"It's how they have to work it, son. Without anyone else, they have to investigate you and clear you. We know they will." He glanced over at Garrett, finding him watching the two of them. "Have you heard anything else about Eineen?"

Grady shook his head as he slumped back in his chair. "Not yet. I'm not sure that they'll let me in. I have seen the police going back and forth."

"They will, Grady. Unless they find evidence to charge you or investigate you further, or they put her into protective custody and refuse to let you in, they won't stop you." Isaiah paused, not sure how to continue. "I spoke with Titus. He'll be around in the morning. He said for you not to say anything more even to Sam at this point."

Grady's face whitened even more at the mention of Titus Matthews, a friend of his father's and a well-known lawyer in town. "Titus? You think I need a lawyer?"

"I do, son. Just for caution's sake. He agrees."

Grady shook his head. "I didn't think, Dad, when I talked to Sam. I guess I shouldn't have."

"Titus didn't think that you had done wrong. It may be to your advantage. But he wants to be present if you talk to any of the officers again. Is that understood?"

"It is, Dad." Grady was on his feet at that point, heading for the nurse he could see coming towards him.

"Grady? Eineen's family is here?" Wilma Wilkes was a friend of Grady's mother. "Come, then. I'll take you in. You can stay for about fifteen minutes. Then, we'll let her folks in about thirty minutes later. You understand she is connected to a lot of equipment?"

Grady nodded, that not of concern to him. All he wanted was to see his bride, and he felt Wilma was stalling him.

"Which unit, Wilma?"

She gave him a grin, before shaking her head. She knew how direct he could be. "This way. Right in there. I'll come to get you when we need you to leave." She watched as he walked rapidly into the unit and up to the bed, not looking around, not even seeing how the officer watched him.

Grady stood, his whole attention absorbed by the equipment, more, he thought, than before. He studied the monitors, not sure what he was seeing, but aware that the readings were not good. He heard the beep of the equipment, the sound of the ventilator that was breathing for his bride, and his heart broke. Why, Lord, had become his constant cry.

His eyes dropped to Eineen's face, finding it even whiter, he thought, than when he had last seen it. I'm losing her, he thought. I'm losing the love of my life, and I don't know how it happened. I don't know why. I don't know who. Lord, I know they suspect me, and I understand why, but please, dear Lord, lead Sam to whoever it was that did this. Bring them to justice. Save my lady.

He finally turned at a touch from Wilma, a kiss dropped on Eineen's forehead, his steps weighted and heavy. He paused in the doorway, agonized eyes turned towards the bed, before he nodded to Wilma, turned away, and walked back out through the doors, to stand at the window in the waiting room, staring out at the bright pinks and purples of the morning sky as the sun peeked over the horizon.

Sam stood and watched, his heart sore for his young friend, but knowing he had to take him in, to question him further. That had to hurt, he thought. He walked towards Grady, his steps slow,

"Grady?" Sam waited until Grady's head turned. "I'm sorry, Grady. I need you to come downtown again."

"I can't, Sam. I just won't leave her." Grady turned and almost ran from Sam, looking for somewhere to hide but finding no place.

Isaiah stood beside him, a hand on his son's shoulder, his eyes on Sam, seeing the distress that was in Sam's own eyes.

"Son, I'll go with you. Garrett's here. He'll call if they need you. Titus will meet us there." Isaiah's voice was stern, Sam looking surprised at the mention of Titus, but nodding.

Chapter 29

Sitting at the table in the interrogation room, Grady laid his head down on his outstretched arms, Titus sitting beside him. Isaiah had been told that he could not go with Grady, that he needed to wait in the lobby. He had nodded, knowing that was how it had to be, but sorrowing that his son was facing this.

Earlier that morning, Sam had stood in Grady's kitchen, a hand reaching for an evidence bag that Alice, the crime scene tech, was handing him.

"Where did you find this?" Sam's words were intense and brief.

"In the cupboard, beside the glasses. It wasn't all that well hidden. If it had been Grady, it would have been stupid for him to have left it there." Sally shook her head. "We found a couple of fingerprints on the glasses that I don't think belong to either Grady or Eineen. They're too large."

"You did? Good. See what you can pull from them. Anything else?" Sam followed Sally as she headed for Grady's office.

"In here. We found a couple of things that were odd. That don't see to be what Grady or Eineen would have." Sally pointed to a picture of a beach and then a miniature clock. "They don't like the beach, not this kind, not that is so commercialized. And this clock? It's bizarre, Sam. It doesn't work, but the hands are set to about when Eineen collapsed last night. It's a collectible piece. I've seen one like it somewhere. I'm just not sure where."

"Get me what you can. Bag that photo and the clock. If they are really Grady's, we can return them." Sam stood, a hand rubbing at his cheek, staring around the office, before he walked away, searching through the rooms. "Sally?" When she appeared, he continued. "Did you find any cameras, microphones, any surveillance stuff?"

"No, and I thought for sure we would have. At least, not in the house. We have had to wait for daylight to search the outside."

Sam nodded. "Make sure you check the back of the yard. Grady seemed to think something was off back there last night.

He's not sure of what. I had an officer do a brief check, but he said it was too dark to see much of anything. Talk to Lydia if you have to. She's the one who planned and maintained his yard." He walked away, his thoughts running rampant through all the scenarios he could think of.

He pulled out his phone as it chimed just as he parked at the hospital, knowing he would have to take Grady in once more for questioning. And that hurt, he thought. Lord, why Grady? Who did he or Eineen make an enemy of? Or did they? Was it one of their family? Jim? Or just some random person we may never place?

"Morgan." Sam listened carefully as he heard Sally's voice, not as calm as it usually was. "You found what? A vial of what? Drugs? Okay. Head in with it. Find out what it is and then let Eineen's treating physician know. This could be it, Sally. We can't waste any time. I'll be downtown in a short while. Find me as soon as you know anything."

Sam stood outside the interrogation room, his mind coming back from the events earlier as he struggled to find the peace he needed, and that was eluding him. He finally shook his head and reached for the doorknob, just as he heard his name called. He spun, finding Sally almost running towards him.

"Sam? We found out what it was. A new designer drug. Heavy with fentanyl." Sally slid to a stop, trying to catch her breath before she could continue.

"A designer drug? That new?"

Sally nodded, watching as Sam stood silent. She knew him well enough to know he was running scenarios.

"Okay. Have you talked to her physician?"

"Just did. He was grateful for the information." Sally paused, sorrow briefly breaking through her professionalism.

"He's just not sure that we found it out in time. He didn't say, Sam, but I've heard the tone of voice way too often. I think they almost lost her."

"I am sure that they did. Okay, here's what we do. Get the word out to the patrol officers. Talk to the detectives. I'll speak with the chief." Sam headed away from the interrogation room, determined to find his chief, and talk to him.

———

Twenty minutes later, Sam's hand once more rested on the doorknob, this time with more confidence that they would find the information they needed to prove Grady's innocence, although he had no doubt in his mind that Grady was just that. Innocent. He needed to get him out of here and back to Eineen. He had talked to the physician. Sally's supposition was correct.

Titus looked around as he heard the door open and then reached to touch Grady's shoulder. Grady raised his head, and Sam drew in a deep breath at the absolute devastation and sorrow on the younger man's face. He was grieving, Sam knew, sure he would lose Eineen. It was still touch and go, but now that the physician has knowledge of what she may have been given, Sam prayed that they would find the antidote and that it would be in time, and if it was, that Eineen would have no side effects from it.

Grady looked up as Sam shut the door behind him before he sat, sliding the folder he was holding onto the table in front of him, his shuttered eyes on Grady before they flickered to Titus. Titus' own eyes narrowed, and then he nodded

"Grady? Do you have anything else you need to say to Sam?" Titus didn't remove his eyes from Sam's face.

"No, I don't. I just want to leave and find Eineen." Grady drew in a ragged breath. "Sam, are you charging me or letting me walk?"

"No charges. Not yet, anyway, Grady." Sam flipped open the folder he had placed in front of him, pulling out two photos. "Can you tell me where you got these?"

Grady stared at him and then at the photos, a frown on his face, his mind almost too tired to think straight. "What are these? A photo of a beach. A clock. I have never seen these before. And I don't think Eineen has. She would have told me, had she. Where did you find then?"

"In your home, Grady. Again, where did you get these?"

Grady's anger flared briefly before he shook his head. "That won't work, Sam. I don't know where they came from. I didn't put them in my house and I know Eineen didn't." He sat back, his eyes on Sam. "Anything else?"

Sam nodded, pulling out another photo. "This. Is this yours?"

Grady didn't look down at the picture for a moment, his eyes on Sam, trying to assess whether he was still a suspect or not. He glanced down at the photo. "I have never seen this before. What is it?"

"What is it? It was found in your kitchen cupboard, near the glasses. We also found something similar in your powder room near your front door." Sam hesitated, his eyes going to Titus, who was frowning at him. "It contained drugs, Grady. A new designer drug."

Grady's mouth opened and closed, but before he could speak, Titus' hand was on his arm, stopping his words.

"Sam, are you saying that this is what caused Eineen to collapse?"

"I am. I need to know where it came from." Sam's heart broke for his young friend, but he had to be the police officer he was, and clear Grady through a thorough investigation, even if that meant asking the hard questions.

"I have never seen these. Someone planted them, Sam." Grady shoved his chair back, rising to his feet. "Are we done? Because, even if we aren't, I'm leaving. Eineen needs me, and God help me, I need her." Grady was out of the door and heading for the front of the building before Sam could stop him.

Titus stared after him before he spoke. "How bad does it look, Sam? I need to know if I'm to be his lawyer."

Sam sighed. "It looks bad, Titus, but we both know Grady isn't a killer. Sally is working wonders in her investigation and testing. She's the one who discovered the drug. Grady didn't let me finish about it. It contained fentanyl, and you and I both know how deadly that can be."

Chapter 30

Finding Grady in the waiting room, Isaiah simply handed him the duffle bag that he had brought and sent him to change. He was still in his suit from the night before, his tie hanging loose around his neck. Isaiah then stood at the window, not focusing on anything, until he felt a hand touch his arm and he reached to wrap it around Lydia.

"How's Grady?" Lydia had just arrived, not having seen Grady since the night before, but Isaiah had kept her up to date on all that was happened.

"Hurting. Angry. Grieving. Confused." Isaiah shot a look behind him, not seeing Grady returning as of yet. "Sam's digging to clear him. But it looks bad, Lydia. Grady won't tell me what all Sam has in evidence. Titus can't."

"The prayer chain is working. Garrett and Esther are on their way in. Eames hasn't left, they said." She looked around. "But I don't see him."

"I haven't either. I suspect he's in the chapel. Some of their friends were through earlier and said that's where they were going to wait."

"I just wish this had never happened." Lydia's head went down against her husband. "Dorcas wanted to come but she has a meeting that she just can't get out of. I told her I'd let her know how things are going. Lois had to head into work, she said. She'll call later."

Grady stood for a moment, his eyes on his parents, wishing it had been different. Whoever had done this had drawn their families into the fray, and he hated that. He became more determined than ever to find whoever it was and bring them to justice. He only wanted his bride to survive. Somehow, in the last few hours, his own life really didn't seem to matter.

He walked towards the doors to the unit, his eyes on the clock, knowing he would be able to go in. He waited for the doors to swing open to admit him, heading for Eineen, standing for a moment in her doorway, watching as the nurses worked around her, their movements precise but hurried. His head turned for a moment as he caught the physician hurrying his way.

"Grady? Good! You're here. Thanks to Sally, we've been able to find the antidote. Did you know it was fentanyl?"

"Fentanyl?" Grady's face showed his horror. "No, I didn't. You're saying you can save her?"

"We are doing our best. Give us about five minutes. Stay right here. Don't go anywhere." The physician moved away, his hand out for the chart, quiet conversation among the medical staff before he finally stepped away, his stethoscope swinging around his neck.

Grady approached the bed slowly as he was motioned forward, his eyes on the physician.

"Grady, we almost lost her a couple of hours ago. If we hadn't heard what it was, we would have. It is still touch and go. I can't promise she won't sink again."

Grady nodded. "God is in control, Doctor. Unless He wills otherwise, she will survive and will have no after-effects from this." He moved closer to the bed, his hand reaching for Eineen's, his eyes on her beloved face. His lips moved as he prayed, an agonizing prayer if one could have heard it before he surrendered his will and her life once more to the Great Physician.

Sam stood for a moment, watching Grady, knowing that he had to pull him away once more, but this time, the news was better. He waited until Grady turned, pausing as he saw Sam, and then walked slowly towards him, Sam backing away as he did so.

"Sam? More questions? Do I need to find Titus?"

Sam gave a quick grin, then pointed towards some chairs, waiting for Grady to sit before he spoke. "Not this time. We found proof that someone had been in your house. Sometime overnight when you were in the hospital. We think that's when the photo and the clock were planted. The drugs? That had to have been done sometime yesterday afternoon before you two had your dinner. The drugs worked fairly quickly."

Grady sank back in relief. "I'm no longer a suspect?"

"Not at all. You never really were, Grady. We just had to interview you, to clarify our findings. We also found surveillance equipment, the nature of which I can't disclose, outside your home. Whoever this is?

The stakes have been raised. You two are not safe, not in your own home."

"I'm not leaving Eineen. Forget that. And to leave our home? That's not happening." Grady looked up as he heard footsteps and then was on his feet, heading towards Bill and Silas. "You two are here?"

"We are. I'm sorry, Grady. We just heard a couple of hours ago or we would have been here sooner." Bill nodded at Sam. "You're okay?"

"I am now. I didn't like being the suspect." Grady looked around, seeing Sam had left. "Now, where'd he go?"

"Sam? He had his phone out." Bill moved Grady to one side, away from the nurses who were moving around. "I don't know if you are aware but my first wife was killed by a designer drug. Cora's husband, who was killed on their wedding day, was one of the ones responsible.

This makes it important that I be here for you."

Grady stared at his friend. "I never knew. You won't have known."

"God was merciful, Grady. Silas, here, he felt the need to come, without knowing why. He hunted me down this morning, just as Sam called, asking that we come, that you needed some friends who understood."

Grady nodded, grateful for friends who understood. He opened his mouth to speak, just as his body gave way, his eyes rolling back as he collapsed, Bill and Silas reaching to catch him, a quick yell from Bill for help.

Chapter 31

His head pounding, Grady roused, not sure where he was, or even who he was for a moment. He twisted on the bed, fighting the hands that held him still, trying to pull the IV that had been placed. He sighed, sinking back down into darkness, not knowing that he was calling for Eineen.

Isaiah stood and watched as Bill and Silas helped to restrain his son, the nurse running towards the bed with the sedative the doctor had ordered. He shook for a moment, his emotions that strong, before he walked forward, a hand reaching to lay on his son's forehead, even as he bowed his own head to pray.

Bill and Silas stepped back, Bill looking sideways as he heard a voice.

"Sam? Did you just get here?" Bill reached to shake Sam's hand.

"I did. What happened?" Sam nodded towards the bed.

"Grady collapsed. His father said he had been in a lot of pain overnight and didn't have his pain medications and refused to ask for any. Given what he's been through, it's no wonder he collapsed."

"He didn't have his pain medications? I didn't know that." Sam's face tightened, knowing that he was partly to blame for that, even though he had had to follow protocol.

"He refused to ask, Isaiah said. Even when Isaiah asked him point-blank, Grady refused." Bill turned to watch Isaiah, a frown appearing. "I know Isaiah from somewhere, don't I?"

"I don't think so. He's a businessman here in town, runs the local hardware store. Why?" Sam was perplexed.

"I've seen him or someone who looks like him around Elmton in the last few weeks since we met Grady. It can't be him though."

"Why would you say that?" Isaiah spoke from behind Bill, causing the younger man to jump.

"I'm sorry. I didn't mean to imply something." Bill looked sheepish.

"No, you didn't imply anything. I was just curious as to why you would say something like that." Isaiah waited for Bill to respond, watching the younger man closely.

Bill shrugged. "It was just an impression, I think. Someone who resembled you in some way."

Isaiah shrugged in turn. "We all have a double, they say, but I am not aware of anyone in the immediate vicinity who would cause you to say that." He turned to watch Grady. "Sam? How far along are you in your investigation?"

"Not where I want to be. Now that Bill's here, I need to talk to him. You stay and have a chat with Silas. Did you know he and Madigan, his wife, had what they like to term an adventure? Being a minister didn't keep him from that."

Isaiah stared at Sam before turning to Silas, to see Silas grinning and nodding.

"That we did, Silas. I found the love of my life through it, just as your Grady did." Silas pointed to some chairs. "How be we sit there? You can still see Grady's room."

Isaiah nodded, suddenly fatigued, his handing reaching for Lydia as she approached, making the introductions.

"Isaiah? Where's Grady?" Lydia searched the area, holding an envelope in her hand. "I was given this by the nurse and told it was for him. There's no name on it."

Isaiah was reaching for it when he paused, standing instead and hunting down Sam, a hand on his arm drawing him back to where Lydia waited, a surprised look on her face.

"Lydia was given this, Sam. There's no name on it but the nurse said it was for Grady. I don't like this. Not after what they have been through. I don't want to see him under suspicion again, not if I can help it." Isaiah sat back into his chair, his hand reaching for the envelope before he passed it on to Sam, Silas an interested onlooker, Bill standing nearby, his phone out as he spoke with Andrew.

Sam stared at the envelope before he pulled out latex gloves, snapped them on, and then opened the unsealed flap, staring down at the contents, before he was on his feet and almost running for the ICU.

"Doctor, who's with Eineen?" Sam was running past him, heading for Eineen's room, to slid to a halt in the doorway before he was across the room, arms wrapped around the woman standing beside her, a hand reaching for the IV line. His movements caused her to drop the syringe that she was holding.

The physician stared at Sam and then at the woman.

"Ellie? Just what is the meaning of this?"

"She's no good. She has to die. He said she has to die." Ellie, a woman in her mid-thirties, seemed to be in a trance.

Sam shook his head, then motioned with it for the officer at the door to approach.

"Did you let her in?"

"No, sir. I didn't. James covered for me when I had my break. I've only been back for about fifteen minutes."

Sam nodded. "Handcuff her and then call it in." He reached with a gloved hand to pick up the syringe, dropping it into an evidence bag, the envelope going into another.

Two hours later, Sam had finally returned the floor where Grady was in a room, nodding at the officer at the door, before he drew a deep breath and entered, finding Grady standing at the window, dressed in jeans and a sweatshirt, his hair uncombed.

"Grady? How are you?"

Sam's words were quiet.

Grady shrugged. "I wish people would stop asking that. I don't know what to say."

"Then tell them that you don't know. Listen, can you have a seat?" Sam nodded towards the bed.

"No, I can't. I'm being discharged, and I'm heading up to Eineen. Why? Is there a problem?" Grady refused to back down from Sam, deciding that he had had enough, that he would go on the offensive and if necessary find the culprits himself.

Sam shook his head. "Grady, I need to talk to you before you do. Your mother was handed an envelope by one of the nurses, directed to give it to you. In it was pieces of a torn photograph, taken the day that you two married. Tell me. Who knew?"

Grady stared at him before he shrugged. "Only my three friends and their wives from Elmton. That means, whoever this is had someone watching us there. It's what we suspected and expected. What else?"

When Sam didn't speak, Grady grew angry, the anger coming through in his voice. "What else, Sam? What aren't you telling me?"

"That someone just tried to get to Eineen again. We stopped her in time."

"Stopped who? Tell me, Sam. Who was it?"

"A nurse named Ellie." Sam stopped at the expression on Grady's face. "Grady?"

"Ellie Bowen? She's no nurse. In fact, I saw her at the camp. She tried to hide, but I recognized her. I couldn't figure out why she was there, with that group.

There have always been rumours about her, that I doubt would have reached the police. She's related in some way to the Duffy's."

"And she's been here in the hospital, just waiting for her chance." Sam's eyes slid shut. How had they missed that? He thought they had done background checks on everyone. Whoever had done them had missed this. He looked up to find Grady missing, the door swinging closed behind the younger man.

Two days later, Eineen began to rouse, her mouth opening and closing as she swallowed, trying to relieve the dryness of her mouth and throat, the swallowing painful. Her lips felt dry and chapped and she sucked greedily at the ice chips placed in her mouth. She slipped away to sleep, real sleep this time, not something that was drugged.

Grady stood beside her, a hand on her cheek, desperate to see her open her eyes and smile at him. He was glad she was starting to rouse, but he had been warned. Until she completely came around, it could not be guaranteed what damage the drug had done to her body or even to her mind. There were too many unknown factors in play. He had nodded and simply replied that God was in control and he had the utmost faith in the Great Physician.

He reached with his foot to pull his chair closer, sinking down gratefully. He should be at work, he knew, but he couldn't go. It didn't matter that he had bills piling up. He had savings to take care of them and sick time that he would take. Jim had been around, assuring him that his employment was safe and that if he wanted to do the paperwork for him, he would gladly stuff a briefcase full and bring it to him right where he was at that moment. In fact, Jim declared, it might give him something to take his mind of all the possibilities that he was sure was filling it.

Grady had shaken his head, told him to hold off on the paperwork. He had been assured that Eineen was rousing and if she continued to improve, she would be home in a few days. He would welcome the work at that point.

A few hours later, Eineen once more stirred, this time laying still as she listened to the noise around her, not sure where she was. Her eyes cracked open and then closed rapidly against the light before she opened them slightly and squinted around the room. A hospital room? Now, what did I do? The last I remember, Grady and I were eating a very lovely meal that he had had catered for us.

Her head turned slightly as she felt pressure on her hand and she stared at the hand holding hers, the ring on it shining brightly in the somewhat dim light. It must be night, she thought, but who is this that's holding my hand?

Grady had roused from his sleep as he heard Eineen stirring, on his feet, his hand reaching for hers, as he watched her eyes open. He bent closer, intent on speaking, when she looked up at him, a frown on her face for a moment.

Eineen tried to speak, finally able to after clearing her throat a number of times.

"Grady? Why?"

"Why what, my love?"

"Why am I here?" Her forefinger on her right hand lifted slightly, but she was too exhausted to do more than that.

"You collapsed on me, my love." Grady struggled to speak.

"I did?" Eineen moved restlessly. "I hurt all over, Grady. What happened?"

"You collapsed, my love. We were walking in the yard and you just went down." Grady paused, hesitant to tell her why. "I almost lost you, Eineen. You were poisoned. It was some new designer drug laced with fentanyl."

Her eyes on his face, Eineen struggled to understand what he was saying. "Poisoned? A drug? I don't do drugs." She looked mutinous at the thought.

"We know, my love. We know. Someone did this to you. We think it was in the milk you like to drink."

"Great. There goes my favourite beverage. Now, what do I drink?" She sounded disgruntled. "Grady? Will you hold me? I'm so scared. Someone has been around in here, someone whispering threats against me and against you. Who was that?"

Grady simply climbed up beside her and wrapped her in his arms, his face resting against her. "Sam found one nurse, Ellie."

"Ellie? Oh, her. Yes, she has always had it in for me. And I don't know why." Her voice dropped off as she slept once more.

Grady simply held her and prayed, asking for healing. He finally rose, heading for the waiting room, where he knew her family was sitting, anxious for news.

Eames met him in the hallway, a hand going out to stop him.

"Grady? How is she?" Eames was heartbroken that this had happened to his sister.

"She was awake and talking, Eames. She remembered up to when we were eating dinner. Go on. Sit with her. I'm heading to find your parents."

Eames shook his head. "They had to leave. Mom had an appointment and wanted Dad with her." Eames looked down the hallway, to Eineen's room door. "I am so thankful that she's better. Having her on this floor instead of the ICU makes it much easier for us to visit her."

"And it makes it easier for someone to reach her." Grady turned to stare the same direction, noting the police officer at her door. "Sam said he has to pull the officer tomorrow. I don't know what we'll do."

"Bill was around again. He has a security team that they use on occasion, if you want the name."

"I'll think about it. I would rather just take her home if I can."

The physician had stopped just behind Grady, listening to the conversation.

"Grady? Can we talk?"

Grady spun, startled. "Of course. What do you have to tell me?"

The physician nodded towards the waiting room, heading that way, and sinking down into a chair with a deep sigh. It was almost the end of his shift, and it had been a busy, stressful, hectic day.

"Doctor? What is it? What aren't you telling me?" Grady was beginning to panic, Eames' hand resting on his shoulder.

The physician's eyes popped open. Dr. Woods, as he was called, nodded slightly. "Don't panic on me, Grady. It's good news. We have the test results back. It was the drug that the police discovered, but Eineen has recovered from it. I have consulted with other physicians, more knowledgeable than I am in this. They see no reason that she will not make a full recovery. In fact, they indicated that her results from today are as if she had never been poisoned." He shook his head. "I can't explain that."

Grady sank back, sharing a lot with Eames. "God. God did this. He protected her. He is the Great Physician. I don't know why she had to undergo this, but there was a reason He allowed it."

Dr. Woods stared at him. He had seen their families and friends praying. He had heard their conversations. "Explain to me, Grady. Explain to me why you had such faith. She should not have survived."

Grady's face lit up with a huge smile as he did exactly what Dr. Woods had asked, leading him through Scriptures, pulling out his New Testament to do that, finally leading him to the cross and the resurrection.

"Tell me, Grady. This is all true?" At Grady's nod, Dr. Woods sighed. "This is what I have been searching for. What must I do?" He didn't realize that he was echoing words from a seeker thousands of years in the past.

"Simple. Talk to God as you would to me. Tell Him that you are a sinner and that you want to accept the free gift He offers you."

Grady and Eames listened as Dr. Wood prayed, tears on their faces as well as his before Grady prayed for him. Grady then handed him his New Testament.

"Take this and read it. Here's the card for my pastor. Talk to him. Call him at any time. And I have a pastor friend in Elmton who would be glad to speak with you."

They watched him walk away, a spring to his step that they had not seen.

Eames finally spoke. "Maybe this is why, Grady."

"What's that?" Grady's head swung around to stare at Eames.

"Him. Maybe this is why Eineen was poisoned. To reach him and through him, others."

Grady thought about Eames' statement and then nodded. "It could be. It really could be." He was on his feet, his hand on Eames' arm pulling him to his feet. "Come one. Let's go find that sister of yours. I think that she'll be going home in a day or so. She won't stay here once she's awake."

Eames began to laugh. "Not a chance of that."

172

Three days later, Eineen moved slowly through their house, just home from the hospital earlier that morning. She was unwilling to sit, and definitely unwilling to lie down, that she told Grady, who hovered over her, following her around until she spun, told him to go find something to do, and let her be. She spun away from him, not seeing the hurt on his face before he did just that, walk away and find something to do.

Grady stood on the back porch, eyeing the yard, determined to find whatever it was that was bothering him about it. He began a systemic search, finally arriving at the very back of the yard. He turned, staring down the lawn, at the back of the house, his eyes narrowing as he did so. Eineen stood on the porch, an arm around one of the columns, her head tilted back so the sun was hitting her face. He knew they would not have a lot more days like this, that winter would soon send them inside.

He turned back to face the fence that he had erected along the back lot line, a frown on his face as he searched quickly before he began a methodical search, his hand finally stilling as he found what it was. His head tilted, he studied the object and then sighed. A camera, he had no doubt. Now, how did the techs miss it? He walked quickly back towards Eineen, finding her half-way towards him.

Eineen walked into his arms, holding on to him, an apology quickly coming from her.

"I'm sorry, Grady. I snapped at you earlier. That wasn't right."

Grady shrugged. "I get it, my love. I was hovering over you and you had had enough of that. Listen, we need to head back to the house. I need to call Sam."

"Why? What did you find back there?"

"A camera. And I want to know how it was missed. That's what I kept seeing, only I didn't recognize is right away." He closed the door behind them, locking it and then pointing to the living room. "You need to sit, don't you?"

Eineen glared at him. "No, I don't. That's all I've done for the last few days. Well, not sit, exactly, but stay in bed. I just can't do it, Grady. I just can't." She stood, her back to him, trying to stand as straight as she could, but the sobs that she could not control began to shake her whole frame.

Grady gave an illegible cry and just swept her up, wincing as he did so. He would not admit it to anyone, but his flank wound was festering. He could feel the fever that he was beginning to run and just didn't want to give in. He knew it was only a matter of time until he did.

"Grady?" Eineen's arms went around his neck. "What are you doing? You can't lift me. You're hurt. Put me down."

Grady simply shook his head and walked towards the office, sinking with relief into his office chair, cradling his sweetheart close.

"Eineen, I think we need to pay a visit to your home in the next day or so if you're up to it." Grady watched the emotions flickering across her face. "We haven't been there since we came home, and you haven't been there since you disappeared. Your Dad and brother have been, but we need to. We need to search there, to see if there is something we are missing. I feel like we are."

"I know." Her voice was barely a whisper. "I know we are." She looked up, blinking against the tears that she refused to shed. "Are you still a suspect?"

Grady shrugged. "Sam says no, but I think I am. The husband always is when the wife is poisoned. I need to find these people, to bring justice to you, and to clear my name." He sighed, a hand reaching for his computer mouse, and shaking it to wake up the computer. "We need to do some research, I think."

Eineen agreed, although she wasn't sure just what research he was speaking of and told him so. He simply grinned as he pulled up a word processing program and began to list names and what he knew about them. Eineen added what she could before her eyes grew heavy as did her head, and she snuggled down further against him, her head resting against his shoulder and tucked up near his chin.

An hour later, Grady realized that Eineen hadn't been answering him and he tilted his head to look at her, a sigh drawn from him. He sat back, his arms tightening around her, as he prayed and then began to contemplate what verses that he could remember on God's compassion, His mercies, and His faithfulness. Somehow, he knew, the next few days were crucial to solving who had been behind their troubles. His head lowered against Eineen, and he too slept, the stress and lack of sleep for the last week bearing down on him too hard for him to do anything but that.

Eineen stirred in the early morning hours, finding herself still cradled against Grady. She lifted her head and then slipped away, heading for a shower and clean clothes. No, she decided, she was not going to bed. She needed to stay awake, but just why, she wasn't sure.

Heading for the kitchen, her bare feet padding against the medium oak hardwood floors, she ran her hand along the wall. Grady had a nice home, she thought, but she didn't know if she could still live there. That would be something that they would have to discuss. She reached for her phone, realizing she had not checked it all day, sending off quick text messages to her family, and then pausing at one from Cora. Instead of sending a text message, she grabbed a glass of juice and then headed for the living room, curling up on the couch, her fingers finding the numbers that she needed to dial for Cora.

"Cora? Am I disturbing you?"

"Eineen? You're home? Oh, wonderful. Bill didn't know when you would be home. How are you?"

"Confused. Tired. Frustrated. Terrified. How does that sound?"

"Sounds about right. We talked about what Bill and I went through. It's not what you are going through, but I can get a sense that you're searching for answers from God."

"I am. Why did He allow this?" Eineen rubbed her finger along the arm of the dark brown leather couch, not really focusing on what she was doing. She lifted her head as she heard Grady moving around.

"He allows things that we wonder at. Bill said Grady was able to witness to your physician and lead him to the Saviour."

"He did? We haven't talked about that, but that is so Grady."

"That sounds like the man Bill and I are friends with. But you? What can we do for you?"

Eineen sighed, realizing that she really didn't know. "I don't know, Cora. We've been busy, or rather Grady has, listing names and anything we can think about them. It's not that long a list, but when I see some of the names, I get such a sense of terror."

"And well you should. Can you send that on to me? I have a friend I would like to pass it on to. She's good at this kind of stuff."

"You do? Sure, I'll send it on, likely first thing in the morning." Eineen looked up as Grady sat beside her, a hand reaching for hers.

———

177

"Thanks, Cora. I know you and the others are praying. I sense we will need them in the next little while."

Eineen clicked off from her call, turning her phone over in her hand, before Grady reached for it, to set in on the table beside her. He just watched her, not sure what she was thinking.

"Eineen? What are you thinking?"

She looked up, her brow furrowing for a moment. "I'm not sure, Grady. Cora asked that we send on our list of names. She knows someone who could work on it for us." She shook her head. "I don't know. It's just I feel this weight hanging over us, like a sword or blade or something, and if we don't move and move quickly, we won't survive."

"I know what you mean. I feel the same. Now, about going to your home? How about tomorrow?"

Eineen shrugged. "I guess. Do we need to take anyone with us?"

Grady grinned. "Sam offered to go with us, but I know he's in court. Eames would go but he's away. Our fathers would like to but I don't think they can. Who does that leave?"

"No one, I guess. We're on our own." She yawned.

"I'm tired, Grady. When will I feel better?"

Chapter 34

Closing the front door behind him the next morning, Grady reached for Eineen's hand, finding her not moving, but staring towards the steps and the front walk. He looked up, a frown on his face, not recognizing the three men standing there.

"Can we help you?" Grady moved to stand more in front of Eineen, sheltering her with his body.

"Grady? Hi. Sorry. I thought you knew we were coming. Bill mentioned that he would call you." The tallest of the men, but not by much, spoke, a smile lighting up his face.

"No, I don't think he did." He handed his phone to Eineen, not taking his eyes from the men. "Check my phone, my love."

Eineen swiped across the face to open it and then checked his messages. "You have it on mute. Bill tried to call you. He said something about three men, names of Abe, Murphy, and Joseph, coming in from Riverville this morning, to help us." She looked around him, a puzzled look on her face. "That would be you three?"

Abe Findlay grinned. "That would be us. I'm Abe, the one on my left is Murphy and the other one is Joseph. Bill called us, or rather Cora called my wife, Emma. She passed on a list that you were so kind as to email her."

"Your wife? That's Cora's friend, the one she said would look into things for us?"

Abe nodded. "That would be her. Now, where were you two off to?"

"We had planned to head for Eineen's home. I know we shouldn't, it's out in the woods, but we need to go there." Grady pocketed his phone and then reached for Eineen's hand, not quite sure how to proceed.

Abe grinned as Joseph spoke. "Then, that's why we're here. We are part of a security team that Abe runs, with Murphy here as his partner. God knew we were needed today."

Grady just shook his head, as he walked down the steps, heading for his truck before Murphy spoke.

"How be we take our SUV, Grady? Eineen?" He didn't put into words what he was thinking but the two men with him understood.

Grady stopped in his tracks, his eyes on Eineen, before he looked up and nodded. "Sure. Why not? Eineen can give you directions better than I can."

Murphy grinned. "Emma gave us those already. She's good. She thought you would be wanting to head out that way."

Eineen slipped into the back seat, Joseph on one side of her, Grady on the other. Grady reached for her hand, finding her cold with fear. He looked over at Joseph, who was watching Eineen intently before he looked up at Grady and nodded. Joseph assessed Grady, seeing the pain he was attempting to hide and wishing that they had Matt, their team paramedic, with them.

The conversation was light, the three men trying to relieve the couple's stress. Eineen stared at Abe, her mouth open, as he commented that the eight men on his team had been through adventures as they liked to call them, as had a number of their other friends.

"That can't be right. No one person has that many friends go through stuff."

Murphy, who was driving, just laughed. "God led us through them, Eineen." He ducked his head to look through the windshield, assessing the tree branches, before he pulled into the road leading to Eineen's home.

"This is nice. But anyway, I always say that God has a plan and purpose for us, that He hasn't shared with us. That' seems to be how life works."

"He could have shared it with us. Maybe I wouldn't have almost died." Eineen sounded disgruntled, felt ashamed of herself, and then opened her mouth to apologize.

Grady's hand tightened on hers, stilling her words. "But if you hadn't, then I would never have been able to speak with Dr. Woods and answer his questions about salvation."

Joseph stared at him. "That really happened?" At Grady's nod, he continued. "Something like that happened with our friend, Ian. He was able to witness to a surgeon."

Murphy parked and then turned in his seat, to study the couple, before Abe spoke.

"You two stay here with Murphy. Do you have keys, Eineen?" She handed them over, a frown on her face once more. "Joseph and I are going to have a look around and search for anything that shouldn't be here. Do you understand?" Abe's voice had grown stern.

"We do. Please. Make sure it's safe for Eineen. After almost losing her once, I can't go through that again." Grady nodded at the look on Abe's face, a question in his mind that he almost asked and then thought better of.

Murphy slipped from his seat, to confer with Abe and Joseph, before he stood, eyes watchful, searching the surrounding woods. Something was off, he thought. I don't like the feeling that I'm getting.

He looked around as he heard footsteps approaching and walked towards Abe and Joseph, recognizing the grim looks on their faces. A few moments of conversation and they walked back towards the SUV, sliding into their seats, with Murphy driving away.

"Wait! What are you doing? Aren't we going in?" Eineen was confused, as she twisted to stare back at her home.

"We're not going in, Eineen. Joseph and I didn't. We need to call in your police. There is a bomb set at the back door. It would have gone off as soon as you turned the doorknob." Abe felt compassion for the younger couple, seeing the fear, no, terror, he thought, that crossed their faces.

"A bomb? They've done that?" Grady was growing angry. "How do we live, if this is what we face? How do we stop them?"

"That's what we will be working on for you. Who do we talk to?" Abe twisted in his seat to face them as Murphy pulled off the road into a rest area, Joseph sliding from his seat to make the call that they had hoped they wouldn't have to make.

"Sam Morgan. He's the one working on it. He's also a friend." Grady stared out the window, his mind racing. "Was that the only thing you found?"

"No. We need to talk to you about what we found. First, we talk to your police department. And then we take you somewhere safe." Abe shook his head at Eineen's protest. "We'll take you home, that's not a problem. Joseph is our security system expert. He'll look around, see what he needs to do, and install it at no charge." Abe's hand went up as Grady's mouth opened to protest. "It's what we do for friends. And right now, that's what we consider you."

"I won't leave my home." Eineen crossed her arms across her abdomen, determined that she would stay and fight from where she was most comfortable. She had been chased from one home. She refused to be chased from another.

Abe and Murphy shared a look before Murphy shrugged. He knew that feeling. They had all experienced it to some extent.

———

Chapter 35

Walking towards his office, Grady paused for a moment, his eyes searching for what had stopped him in his tracks before he reached for the painting he had hanging in the hallway. Murphy had been watching him and reached to stop his hand.

"Grady? What do you see?"

"This. There's something odd about this painting. I can't understand what, though."

Eineen leaned against him. "There are people in it. There weren't before I was sick. Who added them?"

Murphy spun to take a closer look at the painting before he turned, his hands on the young couple, shoving them towards the door.

"Abe!" His call had Abe and Joseph running across the lawn towards him. "Someone has tampered with a painting. We need someone here. Now!"

Grady leaned against his truck, his arm around Eineen, as he watched the activity going on. He was tired, he decided, and sick. He could feel the fever building and knew he had to have help, but he refused to even consider it at that point.

Eineen leaned her head back to look at him before looking around, seeing their fathers and Eames standing behind the police tape.

"Grady? Can we go over to where Dad is, do you think?"

Grady looked around and shrugged, locking his knees to get his balance before he walked towards his father, his white face drawing eyes to it before his father was sliding under the police tape and reaching for him, an arm around him to support him as he slid towards the ground.

Eineen spun, her hands on his arms. "Grady? You're sick. Why didn't you say something?"

Grady just shrugged as other hands came out to help him to the waiting ambulance. Forced to lie back on the stretcher, he reached for Eineen's hand, tolerating the examination. Eineen drew in a deep breath as she saw the fiery redness of his wound before she nodded at the paramedic.

"Can we go in now? He needs help."

Later that afternoon, Grady stood once more in his driveway, the activity cleared but Abe and his two men still around. Abe approached him, a grim look on his face.

"Grady? How are you?"

"Tolerable, I think. They did something that hurt to the wound, stuffed antibiotics and painkillers down my throat, and threatened to admit me." He nodded towards his home. "What did you find?"

"Not what you would like to hear. If you had touched that part of the painting, you would have had the same kind of experience that Eineen had had. You likely would have rubbed it. There were drugs in those figures. How they did that, the techs will figure it out. Who did you anger?"

Grady shrugged, his eyes dropping to Eineen. "Only the Duffy's when I rescued Eineen from their clutches. But this is too sophisticated for them. They wouldn't work this way. It has to be someone else."

Eineen nodded. "That's what we have thought all along. I think I know who." She looked up at Grady. "I'm sorry, Grady. I think it's someone related to Jim."

"To Jim?" Grady was surprised but then he decided, he shouldn't have been. Jim was the one who had sent him out there that day, to find a deer that didn't seem to have existed. It was at Jim's home that he had been shot. "Has Sam looked into that? Jim or someone related to him would be the perfect one to have set me up to take the fall for killing you, Eineen. And I have no doubt that was what they meant to happen. Revenge of some kind, but what?"

Abe had been listening, and having talked to Sam, he had a good idea they were on the right track. "I talked this over with your friend, Sam. He's pushing to solve this, he said. Emma is starting to feed him information and names. Jim was one that she had flagged. But she didn't seem to think it was him, and she knows how to read people without even meeting them. Who does he have for relatives?"

"If we can go somewhere I can sit, we can discuss that." Grady was starting to feel weak, the painkillers taking effect.

———

"Let's head for Eames. He has a good security system in his house. He told me we were welcome to come. And he included you three as well. Unless you have to head back home?" Eineen looked up at Abe, seeing his nod of agreement.

"Not for a day or so." Abe pointed to his SUV. "Let's go. We'll leave your vehicles. I want you two in there, now." Abe shoved them towards the vehicle, spinning as he slammed the door behind them before diving into his own seat, catching sight of the man who stepped around the house, a weapon in his hand. "Move, Murphy." His phone was out as he made another call for the police to return, not that he expected the man to still be there.

Eineen stared at him, her mouth open. "What was that about?"

"An assailant was standing by the house. If you had not moved when I told you to, one or both of you would likely be dead."

Eineen paled at his words, Grady's arm tightening around her. "God protected us, my love. If He had not sent these three here today, we would have gone into your home. He is faithful to us."

Murphy shook his head, his eyes on the street ahead of him, before he cut away to another street, a quiet comment to Abe that there seemed to be some vehicles waiting ahead of them that really didn't suit the area.

Eineen's hand was tight in Grady as she shifted closer, her eyes on his face, seeing the whiteness of it, the dark circles there once more, and feeling the fatigue

in his very grip. Lord, please heal my sweetheart. I
need him.

Pacing her brother's townhouse, Eineen was restless, feeling doomed, she thought. How do we solve this, she questioned? Lord, I don't understand why it has happened. Help me to trust You. Help me to trust those that You have brought in to protect us. We need to come up with a plan, and I don't know that we can. Not in time. Direct our ways, dear Lord.

She paused in the doorway of the spare bedroom, her eyes on Grady as he slept. She had finally managed to convince him that he needed to at least get horizontal and that had been a challenge. She walked forward to sit on the side of the bed, her hand coming out to lay on his forehead, thankful that the fever had broken.

Grady roused as he felt the subtle shift of the bed as Eineen had sat down beside him, his eyes opening as he gazed around, puzzled for a moment before he remembered where they were and why.

"Hi. What time is it?" He reached to pull her down to kiss her.

"About six. I have some soup and sandwiches ready if you want." She bit at her lip. "Abe and his men had to leave. They had a situation come up, he said, that was imperative that they leave. He didn't want to."

Grady shrugged before he sat up, Eineen shifting so he could, his arm around her to hug her to him. "We knew that they couldn't stay. I am grateful that they were here today. We could have lost one another."

"Or both of us." Eineen was growing angry. "I want this over, Grady. I want to end this, but how do we do that?"

"Then, that's what we'll do. I think we're on the right track." He stood, pulling her to her feet, her hand in his as they walked towards the kitchen.

"Did Abe say how tight we had to stay to here?"

Eineen shook her head. "I think he wanted to but knew it would never work." She ladled out the soup, setting their bowls on the table, and reaching for the plate of sandwiches, before pouring Grady's his coffee and her own glass of milk, which she stared at for a few moments, not quite trusting it was okay.

Grady finally pushed his dishes away, leaning forward with his forearms resting against the edge of the table, a finger pushing around a few crumbs.

"Grady, now what? We need access to your computer, don't we?"

Grady shook his head, a grin on his face. "No. I stored everything to the cloud files, so I can access it anywhere. I just don't like being here, putting Eames at more risk."

"Nor do I. We haven't heard from Sam today." Eineen was on her feet, hunting down her phone, frowning at it. "No messages. That's strange."

Grady agreed, reaching for his own phone. "Nothing for me either." He dialed Sam's phone, leaving a message for Sam to call him. He looked up to find Eineen watching him closely. "We need to move somewhere else, and tonight. I don't think it's safe here. Joseph checked the security system and said it was good, but I don't trust it."

"And we don't have a vehicle. Abe made us leave ours at your place."

Grady grinned. "Actually, we do. Dad dropped off a vehicle that wouldn't be recognized as belonging to us. It's an old beaten-up one that has a good motor in it. He had it at a friend's shop, intending to use it for stock car racing."

"Your Dad? I can't see that."

"I'll take you to a race when this is over. He's quite good. He finds it cathartic and stress relieving."

"Maybe that's what I need to do, take that up."

Grady grinned before he stood, reaching for the dishes, as Eineen cleared away the debris and then grabbed a tea towel to dry the dishes as Grady washed them. He finally turned, wrapping her into his arms, his eyes closing as he petitioned God for protection, for health, and for a resolution to what they were facing. He also asked for direction as to what move they should make. He looked up finally, reaching to kiss Eineen before he stepped back.

"Do we have anything here we need to take that is ours?"

Eineen shook her head. "No, I don't think so. You'll find a backpack in the pantry, Grady. I'll pack up the leftover sandwiches, fruit and grab some bottles of water. We can take that with us. Eames won't mind."

"Where is he? He was around earlier." Grady's voice was muffled for a moment as he searched the pantry for the backpack, reappearing with a grin on his face, and the pack held high in victory.

Eineen grinned in response. "He had some meetings, he said, that he had to get to. He thought it would be around eight when he got home.

Let me leave a note for him and then we can leave." She bit at her lip. "How do we do this, Grady? I'm sure they are watching for us to leave."

"I am sure they are. Does Eames have extra ball caps or something like that?"

"He does." Eineen moved quickly to the hall closet, pulling out a selection for Grady to chose from, finding one of her own there. "So, this is where it has been. I thought I had lost it. Eames never said a word."

Tucking her hair under her jacket and turning up the collar, Eineen pulled her cap down as far as she could before she watched Grady lock the back door and shoulder the backpack. They walked rapidly towards a path running through the complex, heading in a roundabout way for the back of the parking lot. She stopped abruptly as she saw the car that Grady pointed to.

"That? Does it run? You were not kidding." Shock laced her words.

"No, I wasn't. I've driven it, so I am familiar with it. In you go. We need to leave." He shut the door behind her and then moved quickly to his own seat, the backpack dropped over the seat back onto the floor behind him. "Where to?"

"I really don't know, Grady. Where do we go? And how long do we run?"

"Let's find somewhere we can crash for the night and then decide. We both need to sleep." His hand rested against her cheek before he replaced it on the steering wheel and drove away, eyes searching.

Eineen was searching as well. "There, that car. I've seen it around your street. It must be them."

"Did you get a plate number?"

She nodded. "I did. I'll send it on to Sam. I can't understand why he hasn't been in touch." She scrolled through her text messages. "Or wait. Here, about an hour ago. He was in court, he said, and just where are we? He needs to talk to us."

Grady shook his head. "Let's find somewhere first and then we'll call him."

Chapter 37

Walking towards the young couple seated at a picnic table in a park in the downtown area, Sam just shook his head. Then, his steps paused before he continued his walk. Come to think of it, he mused, I would be doing the same thing as they are. He slid onto a seat, the bag of food he had in his hand plunked down in the middle of the table, his eyes raised to stare at the twilight sky.

"You just had to meet here, didn't you?" Sam's voice held resignation.

"We did, Sam. We don't know where to go to be safe." Grady's voice was tired and pain-filled.

"How are you, Grady? And don't tell me fine. I know you're not."

Grady shook his head. "Sore. Worried about Eineen. She needs sleep and can't get that."

Eineen listened carefully to the underlying tones of the men's voices, a frown on her face. She finally spoke.

"Sam? What about Jim? How much did you research him?"

Sam grinned. "Direct and to the point. I like that, Eineen. But first, we need to eat. At least, I do. And then if we could spend some time in prayer, I would like that too."

Sam finally stuffed the garbage back into the bag and rose, heading to dump into a trash container nearby, but in reality, he was trying to sort through his thoughts. He needed to get the couple out of the open. It was way too risky. He sighed. Lord, I could use some help right about now. How do I protect them and still investigate them? I know there are some on the force who are convinced Grady is guilty of trying to poison Eineen. I need to prove conclusively that he didn't.

Grady watched Sam closely, seeing the fatigue in his friend, and then reached for Eineen's hand, pulling her to her feet and walking towards Sam.

"Sam, this is unfair to you. You need a break and to catch some sleep."

Sam shrugged. "I knew what I was in for when I made detective. Now, you two?"

"Find us somewhere we can crash. We do need to talk and make some plans. And I get it that there are some who still think I'm guilty."

Eineen stared at him. "Grady? Really?"

"There are, Eineen. What vehicle do you have, Grady?"

"None at the moment. I had had Dad's stock car but returned it. We're on foot."

"Not a good plan, Grady. Now, into my car." Sam felt the hair tickling at the back of his neck and almost shoved them ahead of him down the path and into his vehicle. "You can't be out in the open, you know."

Eineen stared at him before staring at Grady, finding him shaking his head at her.

"He's right. We shouldn't be out here like this, especially not at this time of night." He turned to stare out the car window, not seeing the hurt look that crossed Eineen's face.

Sam pulled into his garage, the door closing behind him before he was out, the back door to the car pulled open, and he was pointing to the house door.

"In there. Rachel's away this week, so it's just us. We are going to talk tonight, and I don't care if it takes all night to thrash this out. It will take as long as it takes."

Five hours later, Eineen's eyes closed and she slept. She just could not stay awake any longer. Sam took one look at her and then reached for the blanket Rachel kept on the chair in his office, handing it to Grady to cover her, before he sat back at his desk, his reading glasses plopped back on his nose as he sorted through the information that Grady had amassed.

"Are you sure you don't want to join the force?" Sam's voice had a tinge of amusement but also distraction.

"No, thanks. I couldn't do what you do." Grady reached for the papers that Sam handed him, sorting through them and then beginning to read, his eyes burning with lack of sleep, but he too was determined to solve it, whatever it was, that night.

"You've done well here, Grady. Along with what that Emma has been shooting me and she has sent myriads of paperwork, I am finally getting a handle on this." Sam sat back, rubbing at his eyes for a moment. "Jim? How well do you trust him?"

Grady looked thoughtful. "I would have thought with my life, but now, I'm not too sure. Either he set us up or he was set up. I'm not sure which."

"I think it was that he was set up. The Duffy's have been seen around town a lot since you two escaped from them. That's highly unusual for them. Word on the street is that they are looking for you in particular, dead or alive. Eineen? Now, Eineen they want alive. I have it on good authority that she is part of a revenge plot against her father. That's what we're working on. Garrett has been helping, but he really doesn't know why. Nor does Esther or Eames."

Grady nodded, a thought crossing his mind. He looked over at Eineen, finding her still asleep, her hand tucked under her cheek, her other hand on the wrist of that arm. He could see the whiteness of her face and the dark circles under her eyes and hated that. This was not how he had planned to marry, he knew, but his love for her grew every day.

"Sam, I have a thought. Listen to me for a moment." Grady reached for the papers that Sam was holding, searching for the ones he wanted before he began to speak.

Grady paused for a moment to gather his thoughts, a quick prayer raised for clarity, and that he could explain to Sam exactly what he was that he was thinking. He wasn't even sure himself if he was not the right track.

"Sam, this is just a thought I have had. Eineen's family goes back to the founding of Mapleview. They have been prominent in the government here in town. Others have been prominent in businesses, health care, legal work, police, fire, etc. They are well respected. I don't see where any one of them has ever been in trouble with the law in any way, shape, or form. We know her father is a well-known businessman, who supports the local homeless shelter, food bank, and whatever and wherever the support is needed.

"Now, the Duffy's. They came to town, what about fifty years ago? They were not part of the original settlement from over a century and a half ago. They have skirted close to the edge of the law and been over it more times than we can count or know about. The current group is the worst. I have found evidence here and so has Emma that they are involved in many different crimes, drug dealing one of the major ones. They are also involved poaching of game in the area. Emma has tracked the family back over the years, and I have no idea how she managed to do that, and to many other communities. They are not nice people."

Sam laughed at the phrasing. "No, they are not nice people. They never have been. I can't tell you the number of complaints we have had about them that we have never been able to charge them with because they simply disappear. You two being held like you were and where you were held has given us a good idea of where to look, but we can't guarantee they'll be there when we go in. And that is soon. Not soon enough, as far as I am concerned."

Grady shook his head. "I have no idea how you figured out where we were. I certainly don't know."

"Simple, Grady. You gave an approximate time for your trip down the river. We look at that, the speed of the river, the wind or lack of it, etc. That tells us approximately how far up the river to look. I understand they are well hidden and may not even be there when we moved in. And that we are planning in the next few days." Sam paused, his eyes on Grady. "Grady, it is crucial that you two stay out of sight. We need you to do that. If you won't voluntarily, then the chief has stated that he will move you somewhere with a police guard. That will curtail your freedom and you don't want that."

Grady stared at Sam, not sure what to think. "I see, Sam. I guess that's what we will have to do. We both need time to heal and haven't been able to." He looked down at the paperwork that he had rested his hands on when Sam began to speak, not really seeing it at first. Then, a name caught his attention and his face whitened more that it was already. "Sam? Look at this. This name."

Sam reached for the paper, a frown turning to a stern, sober look. "That's our link, Grady. Now, I know who to look for." He squinted at the clock. "How be you two head off to bed? Rachel always has the spare room on this floor ready for guests. You'll find clean clothes in there. She went shopping for you two yesterday, said she had no choice but to do that. That God had told her to."

Grady nodded before he stood, pausing as his head spun before he reached to gather Eineen close, finding she just turned her face into his shoulder with a soft sigh, and with a hand coming up to grasp his shirt.

Sam watched Grady walk away, a soft smile on his face for his friends, before he turned back to the papers. He studied them, shuffled them, and then shuffled them again. He still came to the same conclusion. Someone wanted Grady dead and Eineen alive but disappearing, and all for revenge. And that revenge seemed to trace back to the very first Duffy's who had arrived in town.

Sam rose, pacing his office, before he headed out to the kitchen, flipping on the low light over the sink and reaching to make a fresh pot of coffee. He yawned widely as he waited, fatigue eating at him, beating him down, but he was determined to have a plan in place by morning that he could go to his supervisor with, one that he would be confident would work. Only, he wasn't sure that they could even do that. He suspected that the Duffy's had likely moved camp, heading deeper into the woods, and that meant moving deeper onto Garrett's property.

The coffee carafe landed back with a loud clunk on the burner as he reached for his mug of coffee and headed quickly back to the office.

He pulled up his map program and not satisfied with that, heading for the cupboard in the room, rummaging around the find the topographic map Garrett had handed him years ago. He felt it would likely still be valid, although there would be changes.

He paused as he heard a sound and spun, finding Eineen standing there, wrapped in a flannel dressing-gown, her feet stuck into heavy work socks that he knew had been bought for Grady, the plaid of the pajama legs showing below the gown.

"Sam, haven't you slept? It's three in the morning." Eineen shuffled towards him, rubbing at her eyes as she did so. "That's Dad's property. What are you thinking?"

"That the Duffy's are moving in on your father's land, and will likely try to stake a claim as squatters if they can do that. We need to find them, Eineen."

She nodded, her finger tracing the stream that she and Grady had traveled not that long ago before her finger moved back to where she thought the camp might be.

"Here, is this where you were thinking?" At Sam's nod, she sighed. "I thought so. There has always been something off about that area. I know it belongs to Dad and then to Eames and me when he's gone." A sudden look of horror crossed her face. "Sam, who would it go to if Dad's gone and something happens to both Eames and me?"

Sam's keen eyes had been watching her closely. "I asked your Dad that very question one time. You get that land. Your father felt with your love of nature and your work with your blog, that it should go to you. Eames is fine receiving property in town. So the short answer is, you get it. If you die without any heirs, then Eames would likely get it. If he dies without any heirs, then it goes into a conservation area. No one can claim it. Your father has that iron clad in his will."

"If I'm married and something happens, who does it go to? My husband?"

Sam shook his head. "If you're married, and you are, then it doesn't go to him. It goes right to the conservation area, instead of to Eames."

"And I gather this is not common knowledge. They would try to claim land, if they could, or else steal it or force us to sign it over. Can they force us to do that?"

Sam shook his head. "No, they can't. It's too iron clad for that. Your father made sure of that. In fact, it has been that way down through the years. It started with the first one of you in the community. It is a trust that passes down to the heirs."

"I see. So, all this may be for nothing. I can remember vaguely hearing talk when we were held captive, that they were planning on setting up a community up there, and expanding their illegal activities. They didn't think anyone would ever find them."

"But we will and we will do our utmost to keep you two safe and your families safe." Sam paused, gathering up the courage to tell her what he needed to, something that was unusual for him. "As of now, your parents, Eames, Grady's parents, and his sisters are not in town or Toronto. They have been moved to a location for their own safety and so that they cannot be used against you two."

Eineen stared at him before she nodded. "Of course they are. And Abe had a hand in that, didn't he?" With that, she sat down in the chair that Grady had been using, reaching for his notes and the papers he had been sorting through, her mind not on Sam but on what lay in front of her, her own determination to solve the situation become foremost in her mind.

Chapter 39

Bringing his vehicle to a stop in front of Eineen's home, Grady waited, his mind reverting to the day that they had arrived with Abe, only to be chased away by a bomb. He prayed this was not the case today. He slipped from behind the wheel, heading around the car, the door opening as he arrived by it, his hand going out to help Eineen out. Sam appeared beside him. He had refused to let them come on his own. Grady suspected that there were other officers around that he could not see, but he refused to ask.

Eineen headed for the house, walking around it before she stepped up on the porch, her key in her hand, and then paused. This was her house, she thought, or it had been. But it wasn't anymore. Not like it had been. Lord, when I walk through the doors, it will have changed, won't it? I'm no longer the single lady living on my own, with just my flowers and trees and books. I am a married lady now, bringing my groom here for the first time, and under circumstances, we should not be facing. Lord, I need to feel Your peace, Your compassion, and Your faithfulness. I sense that whatever it is that we have been facing is almost over. And I want that, but I don't want Grady to be hurt or our families or Sam or even Jim.

"Grady, what did we decide about Jim?" She turned, surprising the men with her question.

"I don't know that we ever came to a decision, did we, Sam?"

"We did. I'm sorry, Grady, but it seems that he is involved without knowing that he is being used. We have made an arrest in that, but it's being kept quiet for now." Sam nodded towards the door. "We need to get you two inside."

Grady reached for the key to the front door, taking it from Eineen's suddenly shaking hand, an arm going around her. He could sense fear radiating from her and was puzzled. He looked back at Sam, but Sam had his back to them, studying the area around the house, not liking the feeling he was getting.

The door swung open silently, Eineen had made sure of that, and they stepped through, Sam closing the door behind them and locking it. Eineen tucked the keys back into her pocket, and then moved through the house, her hand in Grady's, as she assessed everything.

"Everything is still where I left it. Nothing has been changed. Nothing has been added." She spun. "But why do I feel such a sense of doom, Sam? I shouldn't."

"No, you should. You know you're coming to the end of this adventure of yours. This is always the difficult and most dangerous time.

You need to stay alert." Sam moved away from the door, heading for the back of the house, pausing for a moment in front of the living room. The sudden shattering of a pane of glass had Eineen screaming and Grady wrapping her in his arms before he dove for the floor. He raised his head to see Sam laying motionless, blood dripping down his back.

"Grady, we need to help him." Eineen tried to push Grady away from her so she could rise.

"No, we need to get out of here. Do you have a secret entrance or something like that?" He had seen the slight movement from Sam and breathed a sigh of relief that Sam was still alive.

"No, I don't. I didn't know I would ever need one." She glanced back at Sam, to see him sitting up, a hand clamped to his arm. "Sam?"

"I'm okay. You two head out the back. We have men out there waiting for you. We planned to have them out there. Eineen, I am not sure this was such a great idea."

"I thought it was. I didn't mean for you to get hurt." Horror covered her face.

"Go on, you two. Eineen, you know this area. Find somewhere to hole up. If we have to, we'll bring in a K-9 to track you two."

Grady was on his feet, his hand tugging on Eineen's, as he ran for the back door, throwing it open and then plunging across the small yard and around the gardens she had planted, heading for the trees. Eineen tugged at him in turn, pointing away from where he was heading. He nodded, switching directions, letting go of her hand as she tugged once more, following at her rapid pace.

She finally stopped, leaning against a tree before she slid down, a hand to her throat as she gasped for air. Grady dropped down beside her, breathing hard.

"Did we lose whoever it was?" Eineen's voice was barely audible.

"I'm not sure. I'm not even sure if there was anyone else around. This feels like a setup."

"You don't suspect Sam, do you?" Shock coloured Eineen's face.

"At this point, about the only ones I trust are you, my parents, sisters, your parents, and Eames. We have been watched and monitored and followed and threatened on too regular a basis for it to be coincidence or happenstance."

"I agree." Eineen's head turned as she heard a sound and then she was on her feet, a hand reaching for Grady as she ran towards a thicket, carefully parting the branches and slipping inside, Grady following her, watching as she pushed the branches back into place and then following her again as she slipped into the exposed rootball of a large downed oak tree.

They tried to control their breathing, not wanting any sound to give them away, as they listened to the running footsteps passing the thicket, the curses of the men who could not find them, and the accusations that were flying. Eineen frowned. She knew that voice, she thought, and then groaned. It was no wonder that she had felt they had been followed and watched, that someone had been able to plant the drugs in Grady's house. She leaned close to Grady's ear.

"Do you recognize that voice?"

Grady shook his head. "It sounds familiar, but I'm not sure."

"It's one of the crime scene techs. George Cain. And he's related to the Duffy's."

"He is? Does Sam know that?"

"I have no idea, but I will certainly tell him when I find him." She looked around and then up. Dusk was coming and she could feel the hint of incoming rain in the breeze. "We need to find a better hiding place."

"And just where would that be?" Grady didn't know the area, not that well.

"Come on. We can get away from behind here. There is a small game trail we can follow that will lead us to a small creek and then to another cave. That is, if you're willing to stay in a cave again. The last time, it didn't work out so well."

"It did until we tried to leave. Does this cave have a hidden entrance as well?"

Chapter 40

Early the next morning, Grady stirred, his eyes opening even as he listened for sounds that they had been found. Eineen had led him directly to this cave, checked it out, and then beckoned him in. Both were hurting and not just physically. They were worried about their families and even praying and asking God to protect them had not relieved their minds. He glanced down at Eineen as she slept, stretched out on the hard rock floor, her head pillowed on his leg. He sighed. This was not how he had planned to spend that day. He knew Eineen's birthday was coming up, as in the next day, and he had wanted to spend it doing something special, taking her out for a dress-up dinner, but it didn't seem as if that would work out.

Eineen stretched as she roused, sitting up, rubbing at her hip that she had been laying on, before she was on her feet and heading for the entrance, cautiously listening, not hearing anything other than nature. She turned, finding Grady right behind her.

"Where to?" Grady's low voice barely broke through the silence in the cave.

"To our right. There is another animal path we can take. Unless you know the area, you don't know the paths and where they lead. This one brings us back towards my home but to the front this time." She paused, worry uppermost in her mind. "How is Sam, do you think?"

"All right, I pray. If he had people with him, then he would have had help." Grady followed along behind her, carefully moving the branches out of the way that threatened to smack them.

Two hours later, Eineen paused, stepping behind a tree, her hand reaching for Grady.

"Here. From here, we can see the house." She peered through the leaves and small branches. "There's a lot of activity going on."

"There is." Grady lowered his head to stare at the house. "Those aren't police, Eineen. Those are the Duffy's."

"Then, where are the police? I don't see Sam's vehicle."

"No, not unless it has been hidden." Grady stared around, suddenly frightened. "Eineen, we need to move. I don't like staying here. Where can we go that will lead us back towards town?"

Eineen paused, a finger tapping at her lips, before she turned, pushing him back the way that they had just come. "This way. There is another, narrower path, that isn't used that much. It seems that only smaller animals use it. It's more difficult to navigate, especially with your height."

Grady simply shook his head. "That doesn't matter. I will crawl if I have to, just to get you to safety."

Eineen nodded, finding the path and heading down it, slipping and sliding on occasion on the mud that the light rain from the night before had caused.

She finally stopped, her heart in her throat, as she saw the men hovering around the clearing.

"Grady?"

"I see. Now, what? Do you recognize them?"

"No, I don't." She squinted. "Wait! I do. That's Murphy. Bill. Andrew. But I don't know who the others are."

Grady reached for her hand, searching the area before he stepped out, heading towards the men, who spun at a word from Bill, before heading towards them on a run.

"Grady! Eineen! Are we glad to see you two!" Bill spoke for the group before the men surrounded the couple and rushed them towards the waiting vehicles, shoving them almost roughing into the back of a van, before the men sorted themselves out into the two vehicles. Bill took one look at the two and then reached for water bottles to hand them and then sandwiches. "I don't know how you two managed to elude these men, but they have been searching all around here for the last twelve hours."

"Sam?" Grady was almost afraid to ask.

"He's fine. He was winged, but he's in his office, working on warrants and whatever else he needs. He wants this over yesterday for you two."

"Oh, thank God, he's okay." Eineen's body was beginning to relax, and she just leaned against Grady, barely able to keep her eyes open. She had still not fully recovered from the overdose.

Bill nodded. "He will be relieved that we have you two safe." He reached for his phone, pausing as Grady shook his head. "Grady?"

"We need to talk before you call him. Bill. Andrew. Eineen recognized the voice of one of the men who followed up. He's a crime scene tech, George Cain. He's related to the Duffy's. He could easily have been the one who planted everything in my home."

Andrew's face had grown stern at the thought. "I see. Let me talk to Sam. But we need to get you two somewhere and fast." He grinned suddenly. "You two need a shower, after spending the night in the woods. And a soft bed."

"That's for sure. Eineen stretched out on the rock floor of a cave and slept. I couldn't so I ended up sitting up. Not a restful way to sleep at any time, but certainly not when you expect someone to walk through the entrance and take you captive again."

Bill and Andrew agreed. Murphy shared a look with them before he turned back to the front of the van. He owed Emma a dinner, he supposed. She had pegged that very person and he had stared at her in disbelief for a moment. He knew better than to question her.

Chapter 41

Andrew walked towards Sam later that afternoon, disturbed by what Grady had told him. He understood only too well the gravity of a leak in a police services. Sam had that. Andrew prayed that George Cain was the only one but he had his suspicions that there were others.

"Andrew? You're here late. I thought you were heading home." Sam paused, his hand resting on his upper arm before he adjusted the sling he had to wear.

"I know. I heard some disturbing news that I needed to share with you. One of your crime scene techs? George Cain? Did you know he's a relative of Mac Duffy?"

Sam paled. "No, I didn't. That explains it. That's why I've been getting the wrong information. And he would have the knowledge necessary to plant those drugs."

Sam spun, ready to go find him when Andrew's hand on his shoulder stopped him.

"Wait, Sam. Think about it. If you go in there now, you'll lose your contact with the Duffy's."

Sam sighed. "We arrested them all, I hope, Andrew. As of four today, we have arrested the whole clan of them. George would be the last. Eineen was right. Those two girls she mentioned? They had been there but fled when we arrived. I don't know that we'll see them again, not in Ontario."

"Perhaps not. I wouldn't look too hard. Just let the families know if they don't already."

"I suspect they do. They never filed a missing persons' report on either girl. It is a tragedy, Andrew. Those girls had potential that was stolen from them.

Only God can give back to them a portion of what was lost."

"We'll pray that way for them, Sam." Andrew squinted at the sun, one side of his mouth raising for a moment. "I have your two friends. They're safe."

Sam's hand paused in its rubbing before he nodded. "Good. Don't tell me where they are. I don't want to know. If I need to contact them, I'll call you. Let them know their families are safe. We need them to stay away for a bit. We have some business owners to arrest. It's not pretty, Andrew. It's a real mess."

"I'm sure it is. Call me or Bill when you've done that." Andrew walked away without another word, leaving Sam to stare after him before he too turned and walked rapidly for his vehicle, intent on finding George and having a good heart to heart talk with him. But then he thought better of it. He would let one of the lady detectives have that privilege.

George seemed scared of them.

Andrew slid back into the van and nodded to Murphy, who turned to Abe.

"We're set, Abe. Where to?"

Abe turned for a moment to stare at the younger couple, who had both dozed off.

"Head for Elmton, Murphy. Go past it. Andrew knows of a place we can set up for now. We'll stay with them for a couple of days and then we have to head off. Hopefully, by then, they can go home."

"Sam seemed to think that they would be able to. All of the Duffy's have been arrested. He indicated that there are some townspeople, businessmen, that they are getting warrants to arrest."

Eineen spoke up. She had awakened when Andrew had slipped back in, just had been too tired to open her eyes. "Make sure that they arrest Jim's secretary. She's related to the Duffy's from way back. The connection isn't clear unless you know the history of the town, and Sam moved here when he was young. He may not know that."

"That's the connection you suspected?"

"One of them. Ask me tomorrow when you can tell me who all was arrested. I'll confirm if they have the right person. Somehow, I don't think they will." Eineen's voice died away as she slept, her face turning more against Grady.

Andrew shook his head. "How does she do that?"

"Living in a town all your life, and in a smaller one like this? That will do it. Besides, I heard her family is one of the founding families." Bill shook his head. "I pray they get them all, but somehow I don't think they will. I think she's right about there being someone else."

Two days later, Grady and Eineen stood in Sam's office, facing him, knowing that he had not found everyone. When Eineen stated the name, Sam had stared at her, started to shake his head, and then sighed.

"You're sure about this? You were right about Jim's secretary. He is devastated that she was involved, Grady."

"She hid it well, but I think you'll find she's the one you saw watching me but couldn't place."

"You're correct on that. Sit, you two. I'll have coffee and milk brought in for you. I'll be right back." Sam was out of his office before Grady could even help Eineen to sit.

They were restless, anxious to be gone, anxious to be home, anxious to see their family, but knowing until Sam had made the last arrest, they were not safe. They prayed for his safety and the safety of the arresting officers, knowing it would go hard with them.

A commotion outside Sam's office door an hour later had Grady on his feet, ready to protect Eineen. When it quietened down, he sat back, his arm around her to draw her close to him, their eyes on the door as it opened, questions on both of their faces, surprise and shock on both and sudden fear on Eineen's.

Chapter 42

Bonnie Downie slammed the door behind her, the lock snicking closed, before she stood, back to it, preventing them from leaving. How she had managed to make it back that far, Grady wasn't sure, only knowing that she shouldn't have. A deli owner in town, she had no business behind the scenes in the police department.

"So, it was you, Bonnie. I should have guessed. You always had too much money to have made it through your deli. It never did a lot of business, at least, not the legitimate kind." Eineen was taunting Bonnie, hoping to draw her away from the door. She planned on attacking her if she could only do that.

"Shut up! This is all your fault and your family's fault." Bonnie's face grew more and more ugly and cruel as she spoke.

"My fault? Excuse me, but I just don't see that. Why would you say that?" Eineen shifted her weight on her feet, moving away from Grady as she did so, and more towards Bonnie. She figured she could take her down. Bonnie was thin and tiny and had little muscle. That much Eineen knew from people who had once worked for her. "Seems to me that you can barely pay your bills. Your staff doesn't last long when you can't pay their wages."

"I can pay their wages. They just don't earn them. None of them do. But your family? Pretending to be such hotshots! Putting on the airs! Duffy was to keep you, just like he did the other girls. You were to be given to his son. Did you know that? I want to know how you got away. I paid him plenty to make sure he kept you. Your father and mother deserved to die not knowing where you were."

"Sorry, Bonnie, but God had other plans. His plans are more important than yours. So you see, you still lose. You never had a chance." Eineen had gradually moved closer to Bonnie, searching to see if she had a weapon.

"You were supposed to die from those drugs. We had to come up with a new plan when you two disappeared. You weren't meant to marry him. He needs to die as well. We tried that, only it didn't work." Bonnie seemed genuinely puzzled by that fact.

"God again, Bonnie. He put a shield of protection around us. Unless it was moved, your plans and plots just don't work." Eineen made a sudden lunge, her hands grasping Bonnie's wrist and swinging it back and behind her, driving her to her knees with the suddenness of Eineen's move and from the pain of the hold.

Grady stared at Eineen for a moment before he moved towards her, stopping to kiss her before he headed to unlock the door

"You need to teach me that move, my love. It might come in handy someday." He grinned as Eineen smirked at him.

"I will do that. Now, if you'll open the door and find Sam, I'll gladly turn Bonnie over to him. Then, I think, sweetheart, we can finally go home and start planning the rest of our lives."

"But only with God's leading, my love." Grady pulled the door open, surprising Sam who was reaching out with his key to unlock the door. "Sam, so glad you could join us. Here. Eineen would like you to take control of this person. This person has just confessed to us what her plans and plots were. We'll give a statement, gladly, as soon as you can take it, and then we're heading for home. We've had enough for the day." Grady reached to draw Eineen close, thankful that God had protected them and then provided the ending to their adventure.

Sam simply shook his head. "Eineen, trying out those moves, were you? I am thankful, then, that I taught you and Eames.

Here. Bonnie, you're under arrest. Take her away, read her her rights, and book her for attempted murder for starters, two counts. We'll sort through the rest with the judge and the lawyers." Sam turned back to Grady and Eineen. "I am so thankful you two are okay. George let her in. He's her son, only they go by different names. How's that for a twist to your adventure?" He simply grinned, pointed to the doors, asked two different officers to take their statements, and said that when they were done, he would drive them home.

Six months later, Eineen sang some of her favourite hymns as she cleaned the kitchen after their meal. Their families were all out in the backyard, enjoying an early spring day that had turned out warmer than expected, but that was what could happen near Lake Erie. The weather could be unpredictable at times. She paused, her heart thankful that all was well, that no one had suffered any long-term effects from their adventure as it was called. She still astounded the physicians that she had not suffered any. Dr. Woods had become a good friend, spending many hours with the families, his wife willingly coming with him.

Sam had finally been able to update them on the investigation, and it was how they had thought. George had planted the bomb at her home, the drugs and other things as well as the surveillance equipment around Grady's. Bonnie had arranged for the gunmen, who she had refused to name, and who apparently had disappeared. Speculation was that Bonnie had had them dealt with. Mac Duffy had indeed planned to set up a new community on Garrett's, using Eineen as leverage, but never planning on letting her leave. The drugs had been placed in their home by George, who had also laced her milk with it, not really caring which one he hurt.

Grady paused for a moment, his hands stilling as he reached for the tray with the coffee and tea on it before he moved past it, to sweep Eineen into his arms and kiss her soundly. She still blushed when he did that, and he always ran a finger down her cheek when she did.

"Okay, my love?"

"I am. And you?"

"I am. Finally, I think. I know that we still have some trials in the courts to face, but the last few weeks have been so pleasant. No running for our lives. No drugs hidden in the cupboard. No wife hooked up to every piece of medical equipment imaginable with the supposition that she won't survive. God was good to us, my love. Faithful in hearing our pleas."

"He was. I often think of that verse, the one that you said we had to have as our life verse as a couple."

"I do too. His mercies never fail, nor do His compassions. They are new each and every morning. And He is faithful. Even when we falter and fail Him, He never turns His back on us or walks away from us."

"That is so true." She peeked around him to look out the window. "I am glad we've been able to finally get everyone together. It wasn't for lack of trying."

Grady grinned. "I know. Having Mom and Dad need to go out west for a few months didn't help. I heard from Sam today."

"You did? What did he have to say?"

"He's retiring. Your father offered him a position in his company, setting up security around town and then perhaps expanding. Joseph has been talking to your Dad."

Eineen giggled. "I know he has. Abe told me that. I miss those guys, you know. One day, we need to make a trip over that way, to meet the ones we didn't and meet their wives."

"That we do. And a trip to Elmton to thank our friends there. Without them, we wouldn't be married, I wouldn't be holding the love of my life in my arms."

Eineen hugged him back, never tiring of hearing that. "I love you too, sweetheart. What now, Grady? Are you still going to work for Jim?"

Grady paused. He had had a long talk with Jim that day, and Jim had offered to sell him the business. He had lost heart in it when his secretary had turned on him as she had.

"Actually, no. I'm going to be self-employed." He grinned as she twisted in his arms so she could stare up at him.

"What didn't you tell me?"

"We'll talk. It's a decision we need to make together. Jim offered me his business. He wants out."

Eineen nodded, a sad look on her face. "I thought he would. He'll move from here. He was not responsible for what she did, but he feels that he should have known."

"That's exactly what he said." Grady's voice stopped before he began to pray, asking for the Lord's guidance on that decision and then praying for each one of the people who had been involved in their adventure, ending up praying for his bride.

———

Eineen turned as he finished, her hand reaching for his, as she headed for the back door and time with their families. There would never be enough time, she thought. Life had become so precious to her, after almost losing hers. She could only feel compassion for the ones who had wronged her, offering them mercy in her thoughts. She had explained it to Grady one day in a way that he understood. God had been that way with her. How could she be any different?

Thank you for choosing to read Echoes of His Mercies, the story of Grady and his Eineen. And what an adventure they had. They let me know some of what was happening in the beginning, but like all the others, they just took control of the story, took the steering wheel out of my hands, and took off down the road.

Fentanyl is a drug that has good in its use when done properly but so often now, it is used on the street and it does kill.

It was not planned that Andrew, Bill, and Silas would walk into the book and take over as they did, or that Abe, Joseph, and Murphy would show up. These are beloved characters from previous books. Andrew's story is *The Potter's Hand*. Bill's is *Hidden in the Hollow*. Silas' is *Strong Courage*. Now the other three are part of the series, *His Guardians*. Murphy's is *His Peace*. Joseph's is *His Security*. Abe and Emma's is the final book in that series, *His Protection*. I always have fun bringing them in every once in a while.

I have yet to figure out how they seem to know each other. That is not something they have shared with the author.

God's mercies, compassion, faithfulness. What can I say? They are indeed there, new every morning for what we need that day. His faithfulness never ever

———

fails us. That is something that at times is hard to grasp.

It is with love and gratitude to my older sister, Brenda Bacon Flores, who at my request, penned one of her poems for me to include in this book.

Once more, thank you for choosing this book. May God bless you in your walk with Him.

Ronna

It is of the Lord's mercies that we are not consumed,
because His compassions fail not.
They are new every morning: great is thy faithfulness.

Sometimes we feel like all is wrong,
That we are all alone,
We forget God has been there all along.
He hears our every moan.

His mercies are so great and true
To each of us He bestows.
Each morning all is real and new
Throughout our highs and lows.

We may give up: but He does not:
Each day He gives us more.
His faithfulness is ever brought
To show He goes before.

Although we may stumble and may fall,
He's ever near to comfort and to lead.
His faithfulness is there for us to call
Upon Him in our every need.

By Brenda Bacon Flores
Sister to the author